Under the Same Sky

Also by Cynthia DeFelice

UNDER THE SAME SKY

CYNTHIA DEFELICE

Farrar, Straus and Giroux   New York

Copyright © 2003 by Cynthia C. DeFelice
All rights reserved
Distributed in Canada by Douglas & McIntyre Ltd.
Printed in the United States of America
Designed by Barbara Grzeslo
First edition, 2003
3 5 7 9 10 8 6 4 2

Library of Congress Cataloging-in-Publication Data
DeFelice, Cynthia C.
    Under the same sky / by Cynthia DeFelice.— 1st ed.
    p.   cm.
    Summary: While trying to earn money for a motor bike, fourteen-year-old Joe
Pedersen becomes involved with the Mexicans who work on his family's farm and
develops a better relationship with his father.
    ISBN 0-374-38032-5
    [1. Farm life—New York (State)—Fiction.   2. Migrant labor—Fiction.   3. Mexicans
—New York (State)—Fiction.   4. Father and son—Fiction.]   I. Title.

PZ7.D3597 Un 2003
[Fic]—dc21

                                                                    2002025014

For Chris and Jim—
I hope you recognize your own good hearts
in this story

UNDER THE SAME SKY

The *X-treme Sportz* catalog in the back pocket of my jeans was folded open to the page I planned to show my parents, if I ever got the chance to talk. All through dinner, Mom had been going on and on about the big reunion her family held every July, and how she hoped we could go this year.

As soon as Mom finished, my little sister, Meg, started in on the end-of-year festivities at the elementary school. "Then we do the three-legged race," she was saying. "Jen and I won it together last year, so we've been practicing. Then . . ."

I tried to tune out her eager voice and concentrate on a smooth way to bring up the subject of my fourteenth birthday—and the motorbike I wanted my parents to buy me. I hoped it wasn't too late. My birthday was tomorrow. But I hadn't known what I wanted until that morning at school, when my friend Randy Vogt showed me the picture of the Thunderbird.

I had to make clear to my parents that it wasn't simply a question of wanting the bike. I really *needed* it if I wasn't going to die of boredom over summer vacation. The way I figured it, getting me the bike was the least my parents could do. Nobody had ever asked me if I wanted to grow up on a farm eight miles from town, in the middle of nowhere. My dad was born here, and so were his father and grandfather and probably his great-grandfather, too. Dad's younger sisters, my Aunt Kay and Aunt Mary, had both married farmers and lived nearby with their husbands, Uncle Bud and Uncle Arnie.

I guess none of them minded living out in the sticks, but I hated it. Town was where all the action was. If I never saw another cabbage field or apple orchard in my entire life, it would be just fine with me.

All I needed was for Meg to stop hogging the conversation for a minute, and she seemed to be winding down, at last. "So I said I'd bring cupcakes for the party, okay, Mom?" she asked.

"Okay," said Mom. "You can help me make them, as soon as we get dinner cleaned up." She turned from Meg to me and smiled. "Speaking of cakes, someone's birthday is coming right up. Have you thought about what kind of cake you'd like, Joe?"

I couldn't believe my luck. Mom had given me the perfect opening. "Aw, Mom," I said, "you don't have to go to all that trouble."

"But I always make you a birthday cake. What kind would you like?"

"Honest, Mom, you can skip the cake this year. There's really only one thing I want."

"Oh? And what's that?" she asked, and I could see that I had hurt her feelings.

"It's not that I don't love your cakes, Mom," I said quickly. "A chocolate cake with peanut-butter frosting would be great. It's just that there's this really cool thing I saw . . ." I paused, fumbling for the smooth, persuasive words I'd worked out in advance, but nothing came out of my mouth.

My older sister, LuAnn, laughed. "Well, come on, Joe. Spit it out."

I looked at Dad. His face was rugged from years of working outdoors, and his eyes blazed a startling blue. I sat up straighter and squared my shoulders. Trying for the confident voice I had practiced, I took the catalog from my pocket and said, "There's this really cool motorbike I want."

A quick look at the picture of the black-and-chrome Thunderbird was enough to strengthen my resolve. "It's the one on the top," I said, leaning across the table to place the catalog between my mother and father. "And, see, there's an 800 number so you can call and order it with a credit card."

I watched anxiously while they studied the picture. As the silence grew longer, LuAnn got up to carry her dishes to the sink. She glanced at the catalog over Mom's shoulder and her eyebrows shot up. She looked at me and mouthed the words *Dream on.*

I looked away quickly, hoping that she hadn't jinxed my chances, only to find myself pinned by the intensity of my father's gaze. For a moment, our eyes remained locked.

Then Dad spoke. "Eight hundred ninety-nine dollars."

The words hung in the air, almost as if he had written them there.

"Are you serious?" he asked. The way he said it did not bode well.

"It's an awful lot of money, Joe," Mom said quietly.

"I know, but, look—" I hurried to jump in before either of them could say anything more. "It's got all-terrain tires and shocks and a heavy frame for off-road use, so it'll go even on the farm lanes. And I figure it'll save you a lot of time this summer, 'cause whenever I want to hang out with my friends, I'll be able to ride into town next to the railroad track instead of asking you to drive me."

Dad slid the magazine toward me and folded his hands across his chest. Then he spoke in slow, measured tones. "Your mother, in case you haven't noticed, has plenty to do without chauffeuring you around all summer so you can 'hang out with your friends.' "

"I know," I said, "but—"

"And eight hundred ninety-nine dollars," he went on, "is, as your mother just pointed out, a heck of a lot of money."

"I know." I'd anticipated that he might say that, and had cleverly thought of a back-up plan. This seemed like a good time to bring it up. "But, look. There's another model that costs less." I pointed to the Streaker. It wasn't as powerful or slick-looking as the Thunderbird, but it was still very cool, and it would do the job of getting me out of here and into town. "See, it's only seven hundred seventy-nine."

Dad glanced at the catalog. "Only seven hundred seventy-nine dollars," he repeated.

"I know it sounds like a lot of money," I began.

"No, Joe," Dad interrupted. "It doesn't just sound like a lot of money. It *is* a lot of money. Do you know how many heads of cabbage I have to sell to make seven hundred seventy-nine dollars' profit?"

Oh, man, I thought. *Here comes the lecture.*

"No," I answered sullenly.

"Do you have any idea how long it would take the average farmworker to earn seven hundred seventy-nine dollars?"

"No."

"Take a guess."

I shrugged. "A couple days, probably."

"Guess again."

"A week."

"Guess again."

I felt like saying, *I have a question, too. How many years does a guy have to work on a farm before he forgets what it means to have fun?*

"I don't know," I said instead. Let him think he'd won this stupid little game.

"Well, maybe it's time you found out," Dad replied.

I groaned inwardly. I'd stopped asking my father for

answers a long time ago because of his tendency to say, "Good question. Why don't you get the encyclopedia and see if you can find out?" What was he going to do now, make me research farmworkers' wages or something?

It turned out to be much worse.

"I think it's high time you had to work for what you want instead of having it handed to you," Dad continued. "Give you an idea of what a dollar's worth."

He turned to my mother. "What's the going rate for birthdays, Vivian?"

Mom looked flustered. "Well, I don't know. Let me see. About fifty dollars, I think. Since Joe hadn't mentioned anything special he wanted—until tonight, anyway—I was planning to give him money."

Dad reached into his pocket, took out his wallet, and pulled out two twenties and a ten. "Here you go," he said. "You can put that toward the gizmo you want. The rest you can earn right here on the farm."

"How?" I asked cautiously.

"You can work with the crew," Dad answered. "Find out what a real day's work feels like. I'll pay you the same wage I'd pay any beginner. How's that sound?"

How did that sound? It sounded like my worst nightmare. Working for my father, doing some hot, boring farm job like hoeing cabbage. During summer vacation, when all the other guys were swimming and hanging out and having fun.

I looked at Mom to see how *she* thought it sounded.

Us kids working on the farm was something she and Dad didn't exactly agree on, luckily for us. Dad was always going on and on about the good old days, when he did a full day's work in the fields starting at age ten. He'd have had us doing the same thing if it weren't for Mom. She worried about how dangerous farm work was and said kids needed time to be kids, which always made Dad shake his head as if he didn't know what the world was coming to. But in the end, he always gave in. Or he had until now.

"Joe working with the crew, Jim? I'm not sure that's a good idea."

"Why not?" Dad asked heartily. "He's fourteen."

"Just because the law says children can do farm work when they're fourteen doesn't mean they should," Mom said.

"He's not a child, Vivian," said Dad. "You just heard him say he wants a motorcycle."

"Joe on a motorcycle," murmured LuAnn. "Now, *there's* a scary thought."

I scowled at her, my mouth silently forming the words *Shut up.* She had been unbearable ever since she'd turned sixteen and gotten her driver's license.

Turning to Dad, I almost said, *It's not a motorcycle, it's a motorbike,* to remind him of the difference. But then it would sound as if I was trying to argue that I *was* a child, after all. The last thing I wanted to do was work on a farm crew, but there was no way I was going to claim it was because I was too much of a baby. Somehow Dad had turned the tables. Feeling confused, I kept my mouth shut, hoping Mom would convince him this was a bad idea.

She thought for a moment, then said, "He'd be working with Manuel?"

Dad nodded.

Manuel. I'd heard the name. He was one of the Mexican guys who were here working on the farm. A bunch of them came every April and left around November, when the harvest was done. I didn't pay too much attention, so I didn't know exactly which one was Manuel. Mom obviously did.

"Well, then, I guess it would be okay," she said.

Terrific. I'd been betrayed by my own mother.

Dad was smiling, probably as unable as I was to believe that Mom had caved. "What do you say, Joe?"

"Great, Dad," I replied. If he heard the sarcasm in my voice, he chose to ignore it.

"Tomorrow's your last day of school, isn't it?" Dad went on.

"Yeah," I answered, looking down at my lap instead of at him.

"You can start work the next day." He looked at me, eyebrows raised expectantly. Was he waiting for me to get down on my knees and thank him?

"Great, Dad," I said again. Under my breath, I hummed the "Happy Birthday" song, mostly to stop myself from making a comment that would start a major confrontation. What was the point? I could tell Dad's mind was made up. He really thought he'd made a great decision, one that was "good for me."

I considered asking, *What if I just keep the fifty bucks and forget all about the motorbike* and *working on the farm?* But another look at the catalog picture of the Streaker blew that idea away. I really wanted that bike. It was my ticket to town, to freedom, and to fun—something Dad would never understand.

He wanted me to see "what a real day's work feels like." He clearly thought I'd never worked hard before and wouldn't be able to hack it. Didn't he realize I'd been mowing and raking the yard for years? It was a big yard, too. I'd loaded crates of vegetables for delivery plenty of times. Just last fall I'd helped Dad, Uncle Bud, and Uncle Arnie put down the foundations for the new trailers where some of the workers lived. But that didn't seem to count.

Well, fine. I'd work with this guy Manuel and his crew. It wouldn't take me long to earn enough for the Streaker, and then I'd quit—with plenty of summer vacation left to enjoy it.

2

I was cleaning out my locker at school the next day, working beside Randy. We were both on the junior varsity lacrosse team, so when I took my stick out of my locker, I dropped back and pretended to throw him a pass. We'd just played the last game of the season, beating our big rival, and were still feeling pretty good about it.

Randy, who was the team captain and a great attack man, made the motions of catching the ball and quick-sticking for a goal.

Loudly, I hummed the victory song the band struck up every time our team scored. Randy took a bow. "So," he said, turning back to his locker, "did you show the catalog to your parents?"

I nodded.

"Did they order the bike, or what?"

I told him what had happened.

"Tough luck, dude," he said. "I hate to rub it in, but I made out way better. I told Dad that Mom said motorbikes aren't safe, and he came through with the money right away. I'm getting the Thunderbird."

Listening, I couldn't help thinking there were advantages to having divorced parents. It seemed to me that Randy's mother and father were in a contest to show who loved their son the most, and the way they tried to prove it was by buying him stuff. If one of them wouldn't get him something he wanted, the other surely would, just to show what a bad guy the first parent was. Randy was an expert at playing the game.

"You lucky bum," I muttered.

"So, wait a second," Randy continued. "You're saying

you have to spend the summer on one of your father's chain gangs?"

I squirmed uncomfortably at the image. "They're not chain gangs," I said. "They're work crews."

"But aren't all those guys, like, greasers?"

"They're from Mexico," I said cautiously, glad Mom wasn't there to hear him. She'd probably drag him into the boys' lav and wash his mouth out with soap.

"Like I said, greasers," said Randy with a shrug. "Do they even speak English?"

"Some. They mostly talk Spanish to each other."

"That's going to be weird," Randy said. He laughed. "They could be saying all kinds of bad stuff about you, and you wouldn't even know it."

Randy was always coming out with comments like that. Sometimes I wondered why I thought of him as my best friend. "Why would they do that?" I asked.

"You're the boss's son, right?"

"So?"

"So you'll get special treatment, right?"

"Not much chance of that," I said darkly. I might be the boss's son, but I didn't think my father was going to cut me any slack because of it. And I sure wasn't going to be running to him for favors. I planned to avoid him as much as possible.

"Well, it's not like you're going to be one of the guys," Randy said. The bell rang just as he added, "Not that you'd want to be."

I wasn't sure what he meant, or even if I'd heard him right, but there was no time to ask. He was already headed to his next class, and I had to go, too.

Later on, at lunch, I heard someone yell across the cafeteria, "José! Excuse me, Señor José Pedersen, is that you?"

I looked up to see Randy and another kid on our team, Jason Steiner, grinning at me. "Señor José, *amigo*," said Jason, "why you not working een the fields earning *muchos dineros*?"

Randy, it seemed, had been spreading the word about my new job.

"Very funny," I said. "How many years have you been taking Spanish? You sound pathetic."

"Yeah? How much Spanish do you know?"

"Not much," I admitted. I'd had a little in third grade. When we had to sign up to take a language in middle school, I'd picked French, mostly because Mom had taken it and I figured she'd be able to help me.

"Well, you better learn quick, señor, so you can spic to your *amigos*. Get it? *Spic* to your *amigos*?" Randy looked quite proud of his little joke.

"Ha-ha," I muttered.

"So, Joe," Jason said, "Randy told me your dad is making you do, like, slave labor this summer."

"Slaves don't get paid, pea-brain," I pointed out. "I am."

"Well, I hope you're getting paid a lot, man," said Jason. "I've seen those guys working, and it is definitely not my idea of a good time."

Mine, either. Suddenly I saw in my mind a group of dark-skinned, dark-haired, raggedly dressed people with hats or bandannas on their heads, moving slowly down long rows of plants, their backs bent, their bodies swaying with the movement of their hoes. It was something I'd seen on farms all around us for as long as I could remember, but for the first time I was really *seeing* it. I tried to imagine myself in the middle of that scene, and found that I couldn't.

I shook my head. "My old man says it's gonna be good for me. He's so—" I shook my head again, unable to come up with a suitable word to describe my father. "Lame," I finally said.

Sometimes when I thought of my father, I pictured one of those guys in a robe or a toga from an old religious movie. Like Moses. Stern. Strict. Serious. Always right. Always telling everybody else what to do.

"I can't believe what a lousy summer I'm going to have," I moaned. "He doesn't even get it. He thinks farming's so great, just because his ancestors did it. I hate to tell him, but there's no way I'm following in the old family footsteps. As soon as I earn enough for the Streaker, I'm outta there." I added grimly, "And as soon as I can ride a real motorcycle away from Stanley, New York, believe me, I will."

"Hey!" Randy said. "I just thought of something. Can

your dad really make you do this? Aren't there laws against child labor?"

I laughed sarcastically. "Yeah, you have to be sixteen to work—everywhere except on a farm. Kids can do farm work when they're twelve if their parents say it's okay."

"Well, then, look at it this way," said Randy with an evil grin. "You got off easy for the past two years!"

"Thanks," I said. "I feel much better now."

When school let out for good that afternoon, I didn't get the rush of pure happiness that had always come to me with the beginning of summer. Usually, I treasured the countless days stretching out before me, filled with the promise of lazy hours spent by the lake or at the town pool or just fooling around with Randy and Jason. This year, summer vacation felt more like a prison sentence.

I turned down Randy's invitation to spend "my last day as a free man" at his house after school. I just didn't feel like it. I didn't feel like hearing Jason and him talk about all the fun things they were going to be doing now that school was out. And I sure didn't feel like hearing any more of that "Señor José Pedersen" stuff. Randy was a big-shot jock, and his popularity kind of rubbed off on me because I hung around with him. But he could really get on my nerves sometimes.

When I stepped through the kitchen doorway, Meg sang out happily, "Hi, Joe! No more homework, no more books!"

"Only Daddy's dirty looks," added LuAnn, looking at

me with a smirk. "Man, you really asked for it last night. What made you think Mom and Dad would get you such an expensive present? You should have shown it to me first. I could have told you to forget it."

"I suppose you could have told me Mom would let him put me on the crew, too," I said, reaching into the refrigerator for some milk. "That's what I couldn't believe."

"It *was* kind of surprising," LuAnn admitted. "Especially considering how upset she gets every time there's an accident around here."

We all knew Mom's spiel about how dangerous farming was. According to her, it was right up there with bullfighting and race car driving. She had a point, I guessed. We all knew about farmworkers who'd gotten mangled by machinery or kicked in the head by a cow, or who had worked with a dangerous pesticide and gotten sick.

Sometimes I wondered how a city kid like Mom had ended up being a farmer's wife. Although, come to think of it, she did have another spiel about how growing food to feed the world was the most noble, honest labor there was, blah blah blah.

"Plus," LuAnn was saying, "Mom's been worried about trouble with the crew this summer."

"What do you mean? Aren't they the same guys we had last summer?"

"Most of them. But what I meant was that she's worried about other people making trouble for them."

"What kind of trouble?" Meg asked. "And why?"

LuAnn looked as if she wished she'd kept her mouth shut. I thought I knew what LuAnn was talking about, but I was curious to see how she'd explain it to Meg. We still tried to protect Meg from scary or unpleasant stuff, since she was only nine.

"Oh, you know," LuAnn said quickly. "Some people don't like other people just because they look different or dress different. It's so silly."

That was a pretty tactful way of putting it, I thought. There were folks who plain didn't like Mexicans and didn't think they belonged here and didn't think we should hire them. I'd heard people talk about it, but not lately. Maybe Mom had.

"Well, Luisa has a dress I like a *lot*," Meg said eagerly.

LuAnn and I exchanged a glance of relief. Meg seemed to have picked up on the part about dressing differently.

"What's it like?" LuAnn asked.

"It's got flowers and birds all over it in the brightest colors you've ever seen. Her mom sewed them on. Luisa only wears it for very special occasions."

I was about to ask who Luisa was, but Meg was looking at me and saying, "Anyway, Joe, I think you're lucky."

"Oh, yeah, squirt? Why is that?"

"You get to work with her. And Manuel."

I looked at her. "What's so great about that?"

"They're really nice," said Meg.

"What, they're your big buddies or something?" I asked.

"I practice Spanish with them. Manuel's cute," she added, with a sly look at LuAnn.

Sometimes it seemed as if Meg lived in her own little universe. I didn't know Manuel, but what normal nine-year-old kid wanted to hang around with an old Mexican guy—and thought he was cute?

"Does Mom know you're going out back?" LuAnn asked Meg.

"Out back" was what we called the area of the farm where the migrant workers lived when they were here. Past our house and past the barns, the driveway ended in a circle. Around the circle were four trailers.

Behind the trailers were several acres of woods. In front there was a big, open area with a couple picnic tables and a grill and a basketball hoop and stuff like that, and the old swing set that LuAnn and Meg and I had out-grown. Sometimes whole families came with little kids, sometimes not. I didn't know if there were any kids this year. I hadn't paid that much attention, what with the end of lacrosse season and exams and all.

"Does Mom know?" LuAnn asked again, when Meg hadn't answered.

Meg shrugged.

"She won't like it if she catches you," LuAnn warned.

There was kind of a rule about leaving the workers alone. Mom said they deserved their privacy. I never even thought about going out back, but apparently Meg did.

Just then, Mom appeared with the laundry basket in

her arms. She proceeded to take clothes out and fold them, making piles for each person in the family. "This is going to be your job this summer, Meggie," she said. "And, LuAnn, I want you to take care of doing the wash. You two can share the job of hanging the wet clothes on the line and taking them down, okay?"

"Can't we use the dryer?" LuAnn asked.

"Only if the weather's bad," said Mom. "Hanging clothes saves on electricity."

I knew what she was going to say next, and she did.

"Plus the clothes smell so much better."

I grinned at LuAnn. She stuck her tongue out at me and asked, "What's *Joe* going to do?"

Mom sighed. "You heard your father last night. Joe's going to work with the crew." She looked at me. "It's not that I disagree with his decision, Joe. It's just that I'll worry. I suppose it's silly of me, but . . ." Her voice trailed off.

I felt a glimmer of hope. This was my chance to talk to Mom without Dad around, and it sounded as if I might be able to get her to change her mind—and make Dad change his. I decided it was worth a shot.

"Mom, don't you think this idea of Dad's is a little harsh? I mean, none of my friends have to do slave labor." I didn't like it when Jason suggested I was going to be a slave, but I thought it might help make my point.

To my surprise, Mom looked annoyed rather than

sympathetic. "We certainly don't treat our workers like slaves, Joe."

Quickly, I said, "I know. That's not what I meant. But Randy's dad is buying him a motorbike, not making him work for it over summer vacation."

A funny expression crossed Mom's face. "You know, I don't think it's going to hurt you a bit to spend time with someone like Manuel for a change, instead of Randy and Jason."

I didn't even want to know what that meant.

Mom smiled and added, "Now get out of the kitchen, so I can bake your 'surprise' chocolate-and-peanut-butter birthday cake."

I left, thinking that I was tired of everybody deciding what was going to be good for me. And I was already mighty sick of hearing about how wonderful Manuel was.

3

If birthday dinners are supposed to be fun, happy events with lots of laughs, I guess you'd have to say mine didn't qualify as a big success. It started out okay, with Lu-Ann giving me a very cool motorbike-racing magazine. Meg had made me a card, with a drawing of me zooming down the road on a bike labeled "The Streaker." It was surprisingly accurate, except that it was pink and purple, her favorite color combination. The inside of the card said, "I hope your birthday wish comes true soon. Love, Meg. P.S. Will you take me for a ride?"

The party went downhill after that. I'd been trying to figure out how long it was going to take me to earn the money for the bike, but all I knew was that I was going to make as much as any beginning worker. I asked what that was.

"Five-fifteen an hour," Dad answered. "That's minimum wage."

I'd heard of minimum wage. It meant I'd be getting the absolute lowest wage it was legal to pay somebody. From my own father. No, Randy, I wasn't going to get any special favors for being the boss's son.

I excused myself from the table to get a pad of paper and a pencil off the counter. I needed to figure out how long this was going to take.

"How many hours does the crew work each day?" I asked, sitting back down.

"Ten," Dad replied. "Seven a.m. to six p.m."

I thought for a minute. "Hold on. That's eleven."

"You have an hour for lunch," Dad said. "Unless the weather's been bad and we're really hustling to catch up."

"And we don't get paid for lunch?"

Dad just looked at me.

Oh. Ten times $5.15 was $51.50 per day. "Do we work Saturdays?" I asked.

Dad nodded. "Sundays, too, from time to time. When the strawberries are really coming in, for example."

Mom spoke up then. "Joe's coming to church with us on Sundays," she said firmly.

There was no arguing with that. But working Saturdays was fine with me. The way I figured it, the more hours per week I worked, the sooner I'd be able to quit.

I continued my figuring out loud. "Fifty-one dollars and fifty cents a day times six days means I'll make—wow!—three hundred nine dollars a week. Divide that into seven hundred seventy-nine . . . That's a little over two point five." I looked up happily. "That means I'll earn the bike in, like, two and a half weeks! No sweat!"

Meg cheered.

Dad said, "Hold your horses now. There are a few things you haven't thought of."

"What?" I asked warily.

"Where's that catalog you had last night?"

I reached into my back pocket and handed it to him.

He looked it over and said, "You've got to add seven-percent state sales tax. Go ahead and figure that."

After a minute I said, "Fifty-four dollars and fifty-three cents. Man." I shrugged. "Okay, so I'll work another day."

"Plus shipping," Dad said. "Ten percent."

"No way!"

He pointed to the order form. "Says so right here. But go ahead and call that 800 number if you want."

"Okay, that makes another seventy-eight bucks," I said.

"You're going to need money for gas to put in that thing," Dad said.

"Okay, another two days. So it'll take *three* weeks," I replied grudgingly.

"You've got to wear a helmet," Mom said.

LuAnn, who had been looking through the *X-treme Sportz* catalog, chimed in. "They run anywhere from thirty-nine dollars to a hundred sixty-nine."

"I want you to get a good quality one, Joe," said Mom.

"Okay," I said quickly, before she could start imagining terrible accidents and change her mind about the whole thing. "I'm adding another sixty bucks for a helmet."

"Now, the workers get free housing," Dad went on. "Of course, you do, too. But they do their own laundry—"

"LuAnn and I do that, too!" Meg interrupted, looking pleased with herself.

"Since when?" Dad asked, although he was smiling when he said it.

"Since tomorrow," Meg answered, smiling back.

"Good for you," said Dad. "As I was saying, the workers pay for their own food and telephone—"

This time it was Mom who interrupted. "Jim! You're not suggesting we make Joe pay for his food!"

To no one in particular Dad said, "It's mighty hard to finish a sentence around here tonight." When no one answered, he said, "No, Vivian, I'm not suggesting that Joe pay for his food. What I am trying to do is point out that, although he'll be working along with the crew, he will not have many of their obligations and responsibilities, and I hope he appreciates that."

I continued adding everything up, and came to a grand total of $1,074.53. Okay, so it would actually take me closer to a month. That was doable.

Then Dad spoke up again. "Don't forget, Uncle Sam has to get his share."

"Share of what?"

"Your wages."

"You're kidding me!" I said. "People who make minimum wage have to pay taxes? *Kids* have to pay taxes?"

Dad nodded. "The days when farmers could pay family members or anybody else under the table are gone. Your mother keeps the accounts, and she goes strictly by the book, right, Vivian?"

"It's true, Joe."

I couldn't believe this. I was almost afraid to ask. "How much?"

Mom thought for a moment. "It'll come to about thirty dollars a week. Maybe a little less."

I groaned and started my math all over again.

Mom added brightly, "Of course, since you won't make all that much total income, you'll get your tax money back."

"When?" I asked.

"After April 15th, next year," she said, making a face. "Too late to help you with the motorbike, I guess."

"Hey, Joe!" Meg said eagerly. "Don't forget your allowance!"

She looked so pleased that I couldn't help but smile at her. I *had* forgotten about my allowance, which I got for taking out the garbage and making my bed and stuff like that.

"Good thinking, Meggo," I said, turning back to my figuring. "Okay . . . I'll make two hundred seventy-nine a week, plus ten bucks allowance makes two hundred eighty-nine. It's the end of June, so I'll have enough by the end of July, and I'll have the whole month of August and a week in September left. That's not too bad."

LuAnn was still examining the catalog. "It says here it takes two to three weeks for shipping," she said.

I glanced at Mom. She was looking at Dad. When I saw his face, I didn't even have to ask the question. He was shaking his head apologetically. "No, Joe. We can't order it ahead of time. I made a rule a long time ago never to spend money I hadn't earned yet. It's one of the reasons we're still making it when a lot of farmers have gone under."

"Jim, it's his birthday," Mom said softly.

Dad sighed. "I know that, Vivian, and I don't appreciate being made to look like the bad guy in front of my children."

"No one said that." Mom got up to take some dishes over to the sink.

"The point is," Dad said with another sigh, "there are hard lessons that everybody's got to learn, having to do with money. And it seems to be Joe's time to learn 'em."

He turned to me. "Joe, you clear on everything, or have you got more questions?"

"What will I be doing tomorrow?"

"Setting cabbage."

"I don't know how," I said. I wasn't really worried, though. How hard could it be?

"Manuel's been doing it for years," said Dad. "He'll show you everything you need to know."

Manuel again. I should have known. Just then, Mom came back to the table holding a cake flaming with fourteen candles.

Happy Birthday to me.

4

Making a guy get out of bed at six-thirty in the morning on the first day of summer vacation ought to be a crime. Mom and Dad were already up, and Mom had a big breakfast on the table: scrambled eggs, bacon, toast, and orange juice. But my stomach just wasn't ready for food at that hour of the morning. I slugged some juice and choked down a piece of toast, with Mom fussing the whole time about how I needed a good meal if I was going to be working all day.

"I'll be fine," I assured her. Then she began asking if I had a hat, and had I put on sunscreen and mosquito repellent, and didn't I want a jacket, and shouldn't I take a water bottle. It was too much to think about; I wasn't even awake. "Mom, don't worry about it," I pleaded.

"Your mother's right, Joe," said Dad.

I took the bottle of sunscreen Mom handed me and went into the bathroom, where I quickly slapped some on my face. Then I grabbed my baseball cap.

"All set?" asked Dad, already standing at the door waiting to leave.

"Yep."

Mom came over and gave me a kiss on the cheek. "See you at lunchtime, Joe. Have a good morning."

" 'Bye, Mom."

I followed Dad out to the driveway, where a bunch of guys waited next to Dad's pickup and the big farm truck. One of them stepped forward, saying good morning to Dad.

"Morning," Dad replied. "Manuel, you know my son, Joe, don't you? He'll be setting cabbage with you, like we talked about."

Manuel nodded to me, and I got my first good look at his face under the brim of his hat. I stared in astonishment. Manuel wasn't some old man, which was what I'd assumed for some reason. He looked like a kid, not much older than I was. Sixteen, maybe seventeen.

"I was thinking you'd start in the south field near the permanent pasture," Dad went on.

"Yes. I check the ground out there yesterday," Manuel

answered. "It's wet, but not too bad. So I left the big tractor and the planter there for today." Manuel's English was fairly good, I noticed, although he had a strong accent.

"Good," Dad said approvingly. "So you've got eight workers and Joe. That'll cover it."

Oh, thanks, Dad. Eight workers and Joe. What did that make me?

Manuel nodded. "No problem."

I watched Dad smile at Manuel and slap him on the shoulder in a kind of man-to-man gesture. For a minute, I hoped that I, too, would feel that same comradely hand on my shoulder. But instead Dad turned to me and said, "You listen to Manuel. He'll show you what to do."

Then he headed over to his pickup and started it up. As he pulled away, he called to Manuel that he had to drive to the nearby town of Penn Yan to pick up a part for the sprayer and would probably be gone all morning.

Manuel addressed the rest of the group in Spanish, and they began walking toward the barn, looking as if they knew exactly what they were doing. Even though I'd grown up on the farm, I really didn't know much about the day-to-day work. Thanks to Mom, I'd never had to do it. I'd never belonged to 4-H or done a lot of the other stuff most farm kids did, either. This hadn't ever bothered me before, but at the moment my cluelessness made me feel like an idiot.

Manuel motioned for me to follow the others. Everybody was picking up boxes filled with baby cabbage plants and carrying them out to the truck, so I did, too. As we walked back and forth, I sneaked peeks at my co-workers. They were older than Manuel, which struck me as weird, since he was clearly in charge. It was hard to tell exactly how much older they were, because they wore hats that hid their faces and they had obviously spent many days out in the sun.

I tried not to stare at a guy whose left arm was just a stump. It ended above where his elbow should have been. I wondered how he managed to work.

Another guy smiled at me, showing lots of gold on his teeth. His skin was really dark, with wrinkles that resembled furrows in a plowed field.

I looked away. My face felt too stiff to smile, and it wasn't from the early morning chill in the yard. It was everything: getting up at dawn to work on the first day of summer vacation, and then being treated like a little baby by my father while he acted as though this Manuel kid was his big buddy.

Then one of the other workers passed me and sort of smiled, too, and I realized she was a girl. She had a long black braid hanging out the back of her baseball cap and real dark eyes. Her teeth were very white against her skin as she flashed them at me shyly, before glancing away.

Was this the Luisa Meg had talked about? We'd had whole families with kids come to the farm plenty of times. Maybe this girl was the daughter of one of the older guys.

Was she the only girl, or were there more here? If so, why was she the only one working on the crew? I'd have to remember to ask Mom.

When the boxes were loaded, Manuel slipped into the driver's seat, and the guy with gold teeth got in beside him. The rest of us climbed into the big, open flatbed with the boxes of plants and a bunch of tools, cans of insect spray, plastic jugs of motor oil, empty pop bottles, and other junk.

Manuel drove down the network of rutted farm lanes that led out to the field where we were going to plant. We all bounced and jostled around in the back of the truck. Nobody whooped or giggled the way kids do on a bumpy ride, and they didn't groan or complain the way old people do. They just sat there. So I just sat, too, trying not to shiver and wishing I'd listened to Mom and brought a jacket.

Manuel parked at one end of the field, and we got out. He gestured for me to watch, so I did. The others carried boxes loaded with plants over to the planter and took seats, facing backward. Then Manuel fired up the tractor that pulled the planter and put it into gear, calling, "Joe! Sometimes the plants go in wrong. You come behind, fix, yes?"

Huh?

The tractor pulled away and began a slow journey down the field. I watched, trying to figure out what I was supposed to be doing. There were four big metal circles, or wheels, on the planter with what looked like little rubber fingers poking out. Two workers sat at each wheel, and as the wheels went around, they took turns placing baby cabbage plants from the boxes into the rubber fingers. The rubber fingers held the plant, poked it into the ground, roots down, and came around again, empty.

I began to get the picture. Manuel, the Big Cheese, got to drive the tractor. The others got to ride on the planter in what looked like a fairly comfortable position. They sat in pairs, taking turns feeding plants into the fingers on the four wheels, so that four rows got planted at a time.

Pretty slick. Except that I, Joe, the boss's son, had to walk behind them in the wet, clumpy soil, racing back and forth across all four rows, checking each plant to make sure it had been securely stuck, right side up, in the dirt, and bending down to replant it if it wasn't. Unbelievable.

Let's just say I wasn't chilly for long. Soon the sun was beating down. This was good because it drove away the hordes of mosquitoes that tormented me at first, but awful because I was wearing a black T-shirt. I felt as if every ray from the sun was drawn directly from the sky onto my sweating back. Finally, I took off the shirt and stuffed it into the pocket of my jeans, which helped a little, but not much.

I hadn't brought a watch or, as Mom had pointed out, a water bottle. Thank goodness we stopped at the end of the field after each pass to get more plants from the truck, and if I moved quickly, I was able to get some water from the big jug in the truck bed.

I'd overheard the others calling the guy with the gold teeth Gilberto. On one quick break, after I'd slugged down some water, I said his name and mimed looking at my wrist for the time. He held up his arm so I could read his watch.

Only eight-thirty. No way! I couldn't believe my eyes. I had been sure it was noon or very close to it. Three and a half more hours until lunch. Then five more hours after that. It wasn't possible. I'd never make it.

I hated that the crew sat on the planter facing backward, which meant they were all looking my way. It made me really self-conscious. I couldn't hear much of what they said over the noise of the tractor, and I wouldn't have been able to understand them anyway. But every once in a while, they'd all burst out laughing. I could feel myself flush every time, remembering what Randy had said about them talking about me. I glared at them with fury, sure that he'd been right.

I looked at Manuel, riding along in his easy position on the tractor. His shirt was dry as could be. He had slipped on headphones that were attached to a little cassette player in his back pocket, and the sight of him listening to music while I was practically dying really ticked me off.

The work was so boring and monotonous that there was nothing to think about except my own misery. My mind constantly went over every little aspect of my body's pain and discomfort. This only added to my anger. I was mad at Mom and Dad, especially Dad, for making me do this. I was mad at Randy, who probably wasn't even up yet, for getting a motorbike without having to work for it. I was mad at the other workers, for getting to ride while I walked. Not only that, but I was sure they could do a better job of loading the plants in those little fingers, if they wanted to. It seemed as though at least one plant in every eight went in wrong, which meant I had to bend over and fix it.

The minutes dragged by, and I got madder and madder at Manuel. As crew boss, he could give me a break if he wanted to. He could tell someone to change places with me. He could let somebody else—like me—drive the tractor for a while. It was my father's tractor, and my father's farm. But you'd never know it from the way Manuel acted.

Sometimes the tractor itself replaced Manuel as the focus of my hatred. I fantasized about slashing its tires, cutting the fuel lines, crushing the metal frame—anything to stop the irritating drone of the engine and the disgusting stink of its fumes.

We reached the end of a row, and I was surprised to see LuAnn unloading a big coffee urn from Mom's van. Manuel called for a break, then rushed over to help her set up the urn on the flatbed of the truck. I watched, amazed, as she joked with him, partly in Spanish.

"*Buenos días,* Luisa," she called to the girl.

So, I thought, *it is Luisa.*

"*¿Con leche?*" LuAnn asked, holding up a carton of milk.

"*Sí, gracias,*" Luisa answered with a big smile.

The last thing in the world I wanted was hot coffee, but the others were lined up at the urn, filling their cups and taking cookies from the bag LuAnn had put out.

"You got anything besides coffee?" I asked. "Anything cold?"

"No, señor," said LuAnn saucily. She really was unbearable sometimes.

"Ha-ha," I muttered, grabbing a cup. I filled it with water, drank it, filled it twice more, then threw myself down in the shade of the truck and closed my eyes. I heard LuAnn tell Manuel that, now that she was out of school, she would come with coffee for the ten o'clock break whenever she could.

Ten o'clock? I raised my head and hollered to her, "*What* time did you say it was?"

"Ten," she said, adding, "a little after, actually. The coffee took longer than I expected."

Only a little after ten o'clock. I was starving, but I was too tired to get up for some cookies. Dead bugs and dirt and bits of straw were stuck to my sweat-drenched skin, making me itch like crazy. Blisters had formed and popped on my heels, and my boots were rubbing them raw. The boots themselves were covered with what felt like ten pounds of mud each. My back was killing me from bending over five billion times.

I had earned less than eighteen dollars.

The morning—not to mention the day or the week or the entire month—stretched out ahead of me with no end in sight.

When twelve o'clock finally came, we rode in from the field. The crew went to their quarters, and I went into the kitchen, where the rest of the family was already gathered for lunch.

"Hi, Joe!" Mom said cheerily. "How did your morning go?"

I could feel her and Dad and my sisters waiting curiously for my answer. There was no way I was going to complain. I'd already decided I wasn't going to run to Mommy with my problems. And I wasn't going to give Dad any reason to think I wasn't a "worker," just as good as anybody else. I didn't know how I was going to make it through the next month, but I was going to do it. There was no way out of it without looking like a quitter and a weenie.

"Okay," I said, trying to sound nonchalant, and trying not to groan as I eased my aching body into a chair.

"Your face looks funny," said Meg, looking at me with a puzzled expression.

LuAnn laughed. "Nice job with the sunscreen, Joe. You've got stripes."

Mom was staring at me with dismay. "Look at your chest." She came around behind me. "And your back! Oh, Joe, that is going to hurt like the dickens later on."

Dad's only comment was, "You know better than to come to the table without a shirt."

I pulled the end of my T-shirt out of my pocket and slid it over my head. Yow! My shoulders and back were on fire from sunburn, but I tried not to let on as I dug into my lunch.

It was amazing: I'd never noticed before how good Mom's ham-and-cheese sandwiches tasted. I ate three, and about a dozen cookies, washing it all down with several big glasses of milk. While I was stuffing my face, Dad asked a few questions.

"How far did you get in that field?"

"Maybe halfway," I answered.

"That planter was giving us trouble last week," Dad went on. "No breakdowns?"

No such luck, I thought. But I said, "Nope."

"I'm growing my hair long, like Luisa's," Meg announced out of the blue. "Don't you think she's really pretty, Joe?"

Where did Meg come up with this stuff? Was Luisa pretty? I remembered the quick flash of her smile and shrugged. "She's got nice teeth."

LuAnn rolled her eyes. "Nice *teeth*? How romantic. Just what every girl wants to hear."

"For your information, LuAnn, we're not going to the

prom out there, we're planting cabbage," I said irritably. Why did girls try to make everything about romance? It was so annoying.

I looked up at the clock and saw that it was already five minutes to one. How could time go so slowly one minute and so quickly the next? I excused myself and ran upstairs to get a white T-shirt. Catching a glimpse of myself in the mirror, I groaned at the sight of my bright-red-and-pale-striped face. In the downstairs bathroom I slathered on more sunscreen, then ran out the door.

Manuel and the rest were in the truck waiting. A peal of laughter came from the group in back. Afraid they were laughing at how stupid I looked with my gringo face all sunburned, I jumped on board without a word or a glance at anyone.

And the endless afternoon began. The only thing that kept me going was remembering that tomorrow was Sunday. I actually looked forward to going to church. I'd be able to sleep.

5

I did manage to catch a few zzz's in church before I felt Mom's sharp elbow in my side. After that, I worked hard at keeping my eyes open. I was deeply thankful that it wasn't one of those Sundays when the crew was going to work. I dreaded the very thought of it.

We were home, in the middle of a big Sunday brunch, when Randy called.

"Hey, José," he began, which I tried to ignore. "Jason and I are going to the movies tonight. We'll probably grab a pizza first. Want to come?"

"What are you going to see?" I asked. I was actually stalling for time, while I did a little math. Movies were five dollars, pizza and soda about the same. If I went, I'd have to spend my own money. Dad's rule was that there was no reason to eat out when Mom was making a perfectly good meal at home. As for movies, every once in a while there was one he and Mom thought was worth seeing, and he paid for us all. Otherwise, Meg and LuAnn and I paid for them out of our allowance.

"Probably *Space Ape*," Randy was saying. "Jason heard it's really funny."

I thought about it. Was going out with my friends worth two hours of time spent planting cabbage?

"Hey, José," Randy said impatiently, "you taking a siesta or what?"

"No," I said. "I mean, yes. I'll go." What the heck, it was summer vacation. I deserved a *little* fun. "What time?"

"My mom'll pick you up at a quarter to six. We've got to go to the early movie 'cause she has to work in the morning." Randy sounded annoyed, but I was secretly glad we'd be back early. I had to work in the morning, too.

As I hung up the phone, I looked out the window toward the crew's trailers. Some of the guys were sitting around a picnic table relaxing. Two others were shooting baskets. Luisa was hanging clothes to dry on the line. It did appear that she was the only girl around. It seemed kind of weird. I had to remember to ask Mom about it.

Manuel was doing something to his beat-up old car. His shirt was off. He wasn't tall, but he was strong-looking in a wiry kind of way. His back and arms were brown and the muscles showed beneath his skin as he laughed and gestured to the guys. Anybody could tell he was in charge just by the way he walked and moved.

I tried to imagine how I'd appear to someone who was watching me the way I was watching Manuel. I looked down at my own arm and flexed my bicep. To be honest, it wasn't very impressive. I turned away from the window, not wanting to continue comparing myself to Manuel.

That evening, Randy's mother dropped us off in front of the pizza place at the mall. She would pick us up outside the theater at nine o'clock, when the movie was over. We got our pizza at the counter, sat in a booth by the window, and chowed down.

As we ate, Randy told us the latest news about his motorbike. His father had called to say he'd put in an order for the Thunderbird, and was told that it would be delivered in two to three weeks. "So," Randy told us, "I said to him, 'Two or three weeks! You've got to be kidding! The summer'll be half over by then.'

"And guess what?" Randy went on, a sly grin appearing on his face as he spoke. "Next weekend is my weekend at his house, and he said that on Saturday he'd drive me to the place to pick it up so I won't have to wait!"

Jason and I murmured, "Wow," at almost the same time. What else was there to say? Randy had it made. I tried to imagine Dad shelling out the money for the Thunderbird, then taking time off from the farm to drive me halfway across the state to get it. That would be the day.

I was about to say something to that effect when three Mexican-looking guys walked past the window. Randy must have seen me watching them, because he turned to look, too.

"Hey, José," he said with that cheesy Mexican accent, "are those some of your *amigos*? You want me to ask them to join us?" He was already halfway out of the booth, as if he was going to go to the door and holler for them to come back.

"No!" I said furiously. "Would you shut up!"

"What's the matter, José?" he asked in a fake-innocent voice. "Aren't they your *compadres*?"

He was bugging me, big-time, but at least he sat back down. "Jeez, Randy," I said. "You can be so stupid some-times. Those guys aren't from our farm. There are tons of Mexicans working on farms around here."

"They all look alike to me," he said with a shrug. "You gonna eat that?" he asked, reaching across the table for the rest of my pizza.

"No, take it," I answered disgustedly. How could I explain to Randy what an idiot he sounded like? Manuel looked about as much like Gilberto as Randy looked like me. An idea struck me and I said, "Maybe we all look alike to them. Did you ever think of that?"

"No," said Randy. "Who cares, anyway? Like Tony says, 'If they don't like it, they can go back to where they came from.' "

Tony was Randy's brother, two years older and captain of the varsity lacrosse team. Everybody said he looked like a movie star, and I guess he did. He was head of a bunch of jocks who were the high school hotshots. There were plenty of stories about the crazy stuff they did and the trouble they got into, but they always seemed to get away with it.

Jason was clearly tired of this conversation. "Come on, let's go," he said. "We're going to miss the previews."

As we walked across the parking lot to the movie theater, I saw the Mexican guys coming out of the grocery store and heading for an old, beat-up truck with Florida plates. I hoped Randy wouldn't see them and make another dumb comment.

He looked at them, then looked at their truck. Loud enough so I was sure they could hear, he said, "*That's* why they don't leave—they can't. They'd never make it back to Mexico in that piece of junk."

Jason laughed. I kept walking with my head down, just wanting to get away before there was any trouble.

I didn't know why Randy's remarks got under my skin so much. I'd heard stuff like that plenty of times before. Mom and Dad said it was ignorant talk. I'd never paid all that much attention. It never seemed to have much to do with me.

I didn't actually see *Space Ape*. Not long after I was settled in that dark theater, my eyes closed and stayed that way. I woke up blinking when the lights came on. Congratulations, I told myself. There goes five bucks, down the drain.

6

The next morning, as we gathered by the truck, Manuel reached into the rear bed, handed me the big water jug, and pointed to the faucet on the side of the barn. While waiting for the jug to fill, I watched Luisa, who was sitting in the truck, eating what looked like a tortilla. Was she pretty, as Meg had said?

I'm not a big expert on girls. I'll be the first to admit it. But I have to admit, too, that Luisa was nice to look at. She hadn't pulled her long, dark braid back and put a baseball hat over it yet, and it hung in a shiny rope over her shoulder, a few loose strands of hair blowing around her face. Her expression was kind of daydreamy, until she caught me looking at her. She gave me a quick smile before she turned away.

Manuel had caught me looking, too. He gave me a long, dark scowl.

I felt like asking him what his problem was, but just at that moment one of the guys yelled, "Hey, Joe!" He had on the same Yankees cap and jacket he'd been wearing on Saturday. I was pretty sure his name was Frank. When I glanced his way, he was pointing to my feet, a huge grin on his face.

I looked down. The water jug was full and overflowing onto the ground. David, the guy with one arm, said something in Spanish, and there was a burst of laughter from the others. It sounded good-natured, but, looking back at Manuel, I noticed he wasn't laughing.

Feeling like a real jerk, I screwed the cap on the jug and bent to lift it. I don't know how many gallons that thing held, but it weighed a lot. I couldn't even budge it with one hand. Grabbing the handle with both hands, I held it up in front of me, leaned back against the weight of it, and taking ridiculous little shuffle steps, I finally got it over to the truck.

I knew my face was flaming red from exertion and embarrassment—and anger. I was sure Manuel had wanted me to look foolish in front of the whole crew. The memory of his muscled arms made me even madder somehow, but that gave me strength and determination. With a giant effort, I hoisted the jug up onto the open tailgate of the truck.

Dad came out of the house then to speak with Manuel. The sight of them talking seriously, man-to-man, did nothing to ease the tightness in my chest. Then Manuel was gesturing and Dad was nodding, and Dad let out a big smile and shook Manuel's hand. I looked away until I heard Manuel come back over to the truck.

When everyone else started climbing aboard, I did, too. I sat like a stone, not saying anything to anybody as we rode bumpily to the same field we'd been in on Saturday. Manuel didn't order any change in positions, so I took my place behind the planter, and the agony began again.

Everything went along as boringly and painfully as it had on Saturday, until somewhere around two o'clock that afternoon. We were on a break at the end of a row. Two of the guys were messing with a little transistor radio, trying to get a station with Spanish music. One had introduced himself as Jorge, the other had told me his name was Carlos. Jorge was kind of chubby, and Carlos was taller than everybody else, including me, though most of the guys were shorter. Standing with them was a guy who looked pretty old.

There was another guy whose name was Rafael, but

half the time the others called him Mula. They were teasing when they said it, busting him for being lazy. I'd noticed that he tried to get away with slacking off whenever he could. Manuel was always coming up behind him and pretending to kick him in the rear. It didn't take any genius on my part to figure out that *mula* meant "mule."

They used nicknames a lot. Sometimes they called David, the one-armed guy, Rechoncho. I figured it meant "stumpy" or something like that. It wasn't that they were making fun of him. They just didn't try to ignore his injury or pretend it hadn't happened, which is the way most people I knew would have acted.

They called Manuel Capitán, not sarcastically, but in a friendly and respectful way. They had a whole bunch of affectionate-sounding nicknames for Luisa. I was just Joe.

Sort of halfway paying attention to what Jorge and Carlos were doing with the radio, I started pouring myself water from the jug. All at once, the air was filled with terrified screams. Luisa came bursting out from behind the hedgerow that divided the fields, her arms pinwheeling around her head, her hands batting at a huge cloud of ticked-off, stinging hornets.

Everyone began yelling in Spanish. I didn't know what they were telling her to do, but it was obvious that she was way too panicked to listen to their advice. We all stood helplessly by while she raced around the field shrieking and swatting at the air and trying unsuccessfully to escape.

It was unbearable to watch, but none of us seemed

able to turn away, either. Then Luisa tripped on the unevenly plowed earth and fell face down with a loud *whump*. Manuel ran over and threw himself on top of her, trying to protect her body with his as the hornets continued to swarm.

Then I remembered seeing a can of hornet spray rolling around in the bed of the truck with all the tools and other junk, and I hurried to get it. I'd used the stuff before to bomb wasps and their nests, but I'd never sprayed it at insects that were attacking people. It was poison. Was it poisonous to humans? I hesitated.

But the sound of Luisa sobbing and the sight of Manuel and her lying there with yellow jackets buzzing all around them were too horrifying. I had to do something. So I stepped closer, hollering, "Close your eyes and your mouths—tight!" And I let rip with the spray bomb.

Twitching insects fell all over the place and quickly died. Some flew off, and I sincerely hoped they were going somewhere to die, too. The world became very quiet.

"Are you guys okay?" I called shakily.

Manuel straightened his arms, looked down at Luisa, and said something in Spanish. She answered, also in Spanish, crying as she spoke. She sat up and swatted at the carcasses of insects that lay on and around her.

"Careful!" I shouted. "They might not all be dead!" I grabbed her arm to pull her to her feet and away from the fumes and the hornet bodies. Manuel followed, choking— probably from the spray he had breathed.

He held Luisa's face gently in both his hands and examined it. Even from where I stood, I could see the swelling and sore-looking red spots. I could tell, too, that Luisa was trying to say she was fine, even though her eyes were swelling shut as we watched. Suddenly she sort of slumped, and Manuel caught her.

For a terrible moment I was afraid she was dead, then realized that she must have fainted. Manuel had lifted Luisa up and was carrying her over to the truck, shouting in Spanish. I'd never seen an unconscious person before and I was really freaked out, so it took me a minute to realize Manuel was talking to me as he laid Luisa down on the front seat.

"English!" I shouted back. "Speak English!"

Manuel was so upset that at first he just stared at me, then he seemed to hear what I was saying. "You—take the truck. Hurry! *Su madre*—" He shook his head and switched back to English. "Your mother. She fix Luisa, *sí*? She knows how to do. Hurry!"

"*You* take her!" I said. "You drive! Go!" The idea of being the one responsible for getting Luisa to safety scared me.

For a few seconds, Manuel looked unsure. Then he said, "No. Your mother, you can tell her everything. You go. I stay." He looked at me frantically as if he were willing me to understand something.

There wasn't time to argue about it, that was for sure. "Okay," I said loudly. "I'll go. Okay," I repeated, trying to be calm as I got behind the wheel of the truck. Every farm kid, even one like me who hadn't done much work around the place, knew how to drive a truck or a tractor. I didn't have a license or anything, but I was allowed to go anywhere on our land and on the farm lanes.

I had never been behind the wheel of that big truck before, though, and I'd sure never driven with a girl in a dead faint on the seat beside me, and I was really nervous. Things I'd heard about allergies to bees kept racing through my head. I knew if someone was having as bad a reaction as Luisa was, there wasn't much time. People could die from insect stings if they didn't get help quickly.

Thinking about that didn't do anything to calm me down. I felt even clumsier than usual, fumbling with the keys, then stalling, not once but three times before I got the stupid truck going.

It was no comfort that all the guys were standing there watching and waiting, and that Manuel looked ready to jump out of his skin. Couldn't he see I was hurrying as fast as I could?

I tried to concentrate on finding the gears, and soon I was lurching down the lane toward home. Poor Luisa was bouncing around on the seat and practically sliding onto the floor, but I couldn't do anything about it. I had to keep both hands on the wheel to steer through the deep ruts in the road.

As I pulled up next to the house, I honked the horn and hollered for Mom. She rushed out, and together we carried Luisa into the house and placed her on the couch. The whole time, Mom was asking questions and I was answering them the best I could. The really scary thing was that Luisa's neck had started to swell also, and her breathing was beginning to sound strangled, as if her throat was closing up, too.

Mom ran for the first aid kit, leaving me there with Luisa, and I kept saying, "Don't die don't die don't die don't die," until Mom got back. She had something in her hand that looked like a pen, but that I later found out was a syringe with a drug for people who were allergic to bee stings.

Mom stabbed the end of the pen into Luisa's arm, and almost immediately Luisa's breathing became easier and more even. Then Mom asked me to get a big plastic bowl from the kitchen in case Luisa felt sick to her stomach.

When I got back, Mom was using little tweezers to remove all the stingers that were stuck in Luisa's skin. She mixed baking soda with cold water and spread it over the red spots, and covered the worst places with plastic bags full of ice. She put a washcloth over Luisa's eyes, and an ice bag on top of that. The whole time she never stopped talking to Luisa, who was awake but still woozy. Mom kept saying, "Lie still. Just rest. The worst is over."

While Mom dialed 911, I got a drink of water and tried to settle down. Mom told the person on the other end of the line what had happened and what she had done.

"Yes, she seems to be breathing quite well now," Mom said. "Yes, the swelling's going down. No, no vomiting. Pretty alert, yes. No. No. Yes. Okay, then, thank you."

When she hung up, she looked relieved. "It sounds as if you're going to be just fine, Luisa." Then she murmured, almost to herself, "Jim teases me for worrying about accidents, but you just never know . . ."

To my dismay, she turned to me and said, "As soon as you finish that drink, Joe, you'd better get back out to the field and tell Manuel she's all right. He must be worried sick."

A look of concern passed over her face then and she said, "He got stung, too, didn't he? You tell him to come back here right away if he's feeling the least bit strange, all right?"

"Okay."

"Why didn't he drive Luisa himself?" she asked then.

"I don't know. I tried to get him to do it, but he told *me* to."

Luisa spoke up in a weak voice. "He probably thought he should keep working. You know, 'cause he's crew boss."

"For goodness' sake," Mom said, shaking her head with a mix of admiration and exasperation. "That's just like him. Now, Joe, you go tell him Luisa is going to be just fine, and that I'll keep her here with me until he gets back."

"Okay," I said reluctantly, thinking that I was obviously not as dedicated to work as the great Manuel. I wouldn't have wished a hornet attack on Luisa or anybody else, believe me. But now that it had happened, I'd been secretly hoping it would give me an excuse to stay home. Playing Nurse Joe and sitting beside a sick girl was not something I'd ordinarily volunteer for, but it was a lot more appealing than going back to the cabbage field.

When I got there, Manuel practically leaped off the tractor and started asking a million questions about Luisa. Finally, he seemed convinced that she was really okay. He had a lot of red welts on his face and arms, but he didn't look anywhere near as bad as Luisa, and he waved me off when I repeated Mom's offer to go back to the house for first aid.

Fortunately, there had to be an even number of people feeding the wheels on the planter, so I got to take Luisa's place next to Gilberto. Halfway down each row, Manuel stopped the tractor and we all took turns jumping off the planter to go back and do the job of checking the plants. That was better, but not much. Feeding the plants into the rubber fingers looked easy, but it took me a while to get the hang of it.

After a period of time that felt like days instead of hours, we left the field and bounced back to our driveway. Manuel followed me right over to our house, but hesitated at the kitchen door for a moment, as if he wasn't sure he should come inside. It was the second time that day I'd seen Manuel unsure of himself. I wondered if the real reason he hadn't wanted to drive Luisa here was that he didn't feel right about barging into our house and yelling for Mom to do something, even in an emergency. I hadn't thought of that at the time, but, looking at Manuel now, I suspected I was right.

For a second or two I paused, enjoying Manuel's discomfort. Then I took pity on him. "Come on in," I said. Hearing voices in the living room, I motioned for Manuel to follow me.

Luisa was sitting up now, laughing and talking with Meg and LuAnn. She didn't look so hot, with her blotchy red swollen face covered with white dabs of Mom's magic potion. But she told Manuel she felt much better.

"I work tomorrow, no problem," she said earnestly to him.

He scowled and murmured something in Spanish that probably meant, "We'll see about that."

Mom came in then and looked Manuel over. She dabbed some of the white stuff on his blotches, and gave him some to take back to the trailer to use on Luisa later. Then she gave him a box of syringes. "From now on, one of these stays in the glove compartment of each truck," she said. To Luisa she said, "Is this the first time you've had a reaction like this?"

Luisa nodded.

"I don't want to scare you, but the next one could be even worse. You should carry a syringe with you whenever you can." Then, gently but seriously, she added, "And from now on, when you go through the hedgerows you'll have to be extra careful, okay?"

Luisa looked down. She was embarrassed, I could tell, though Mom hadn't meant to make her feel bad. It was a fact of life that sometimes we had to pee when we were working, and we just went behind the rows of bushes between fields. That was what Luisa had been doing when she stirred up the hornets' nest.

Manuel stepped up and took her gently by the arm to leave. "I work tomorrow, no problem," Luisa repeated to Mom.

"Let's wait and see how you feel," Mom answered.

After thanking Mom about a hundred times, Manuel and Luisa left.

Naturally, Luisa's accident was the main topic of conversation at the dinner table that night. While everyone talked about how scary it must have been, and how lucky Luisa was that Mom was there and knew what to do, I mulled over something that had been on my mind ever since I'd known Luisa was going to be okay.

All of us on the crew had been upset by Luisa's accident, but Manuel had acted really crazy. I kept seeing him throw himself over Luisa's fallen body, and remembered how desperately he'd questioned me about how she was doing. I recalled, too, the black stare he'd given me that morning when he found me looking at her.

When there was a lull in the conversation, I asked, "Is Luisa Manuel's girlfriend or something?"

Everyone at the table looked at me as if my head had turned into a cabbage or something.

"*What?*" I demanded.

"She's his *cousin,* pea-brain," LuAnn said. "You've worked with them for two whole days and you never figured that out?" She shook her head.

Feeling obligated to defend myself, I said in a tone as snotty as hers, "For your information, *pea-brain,* that's exactly what we were doing: *working.* We weren't out there comparing family trees."

"Stop it right now, you two," said Mom. To LuAnn she said, "Joe wouldn't necessarily know they were cousins." To me she said, "Manuel feels very responsible for Luisa, because she's young, and a girl, and so far from home."

I'd been meaning to ask about that. "How come she's the only girl here, anyway?"

Mom shrugged and said, "Her family needs the money she's earning."

"Doesn't she have parents?" I asked. "Don't they have jobs?"

"Well, yes," Mom answered. "But they're back in Mexico. They can't make much there."

"She misses them," Meg piped up. "She told me."

"I'm sure she does, honey," said Mom. To me she said, "When Manuel was getting the crew together, he told

Luisa's family about us, that we would treat Luisa well. So here she is."

LuAnn had been itching to say something. She wasn't about to let me off the hook for being dense. "Mom, Manuel and his family have been coming here for— what?—ten years or something?"

"Eleven," Dad answered.

"Eleven years," LuAnn repeated, with a significant look in my direction. "So wouldn't you think Joe would at least have a clue—"

Mom cut her off with a sharp glance.

"But *Luisa's* never been here before, right?" I pointed out. "So how was I supposed to know she was Manuel's cousin?"

"You're right, Joe," said Mom. "This is Luisa's first time with us. Victor started with us when Manuel was only five."

Risking another outburst of ridicule, I asked, "Who's Victor?"

LuAnn sighed loudly, and Mom gave her a warning glance. "Victor is Manuel's father," she answered. "He used to be crew boss."

"So where is he?"

"He's in Mexico, too. He hurt his back picking apples on another job after he left here last year. María—that's his wife, Manuel's mother—had to stay home to take care of him." Mom looked troubled. "It's been tough for them.

Victor's injury is serious, and he has no health insurance. He may never work again."

Mom stood up and began clearing the table as she talked. "We didn't know all this until Manuel showed up at the beginning of the season and asked your father if he could take his father's place as crew boss."

"I didn't even have to think it over," Dad said. "Manuel has been working since he was a little boy. I knew he'd do a good job, and he needs the extra money, now that he's supporting the whole family. There are two little brothers and a sister back in Mexico."

"Luisa has three little sisters and a brother at home," Meg said. "That's why they need money. But it's sad. She had to leave school 'cause she's the oldest."

"Wait a second," I said. "How old is she?"

"The same as you," LuAnn said. "Fourteen. And Manuel's sixteen, same as me."

Whoa. I was trying to take that in when Meg looked from LuAnn to me and said, "They seem older than you guys."

Which was exactly what I'd been thinking, but hadn't wanted to say.

"Some children have to grow up very fast," Mom said.

Dad said, "You've got to admire a young man Manuel's age who's shouldering the kind of responsibility he's got."

I couldn't imagine being two years older than I was and taking care of my whole family, including my parents.

And even though, like most kids, I complained about having to go to school, I wouldn't want to be forced to quit and go to work, as Manuel and Luisa had had to do. I planned to go to college someday and never do farm work again.

And okay, Manuel was doing a big job for a sixteen-year-old kid. But I thought I had been fairly heroic myself that afternoon, spraying the hornets and driving Luisa to safety and all, yet nobody had said a word to me about it. I'd heard about how great Mom was with first aid, and how brave Luisa was, and how responsible and mature Manuel was, but I wasn't worth mentioning.

At least, that was what my family, especially my father, seemed to think.

7

Luisa came back to work the next day, as she'd said she would. She was still a little swollen and blotchy-looking, but not too bad, and she acted perfectly normal. At least, I was pretty sure she did. I was almost afraid to look at her with Manuel hovering around all the time.

The aches in my body hadn't gone away; they might even have been worse than when I started. I looked for visible signs of the new muscles I could feel so acutely, but my arms and legs looked the same as ever. The good news was that I'd recovered from the sunburn, and my embarrassing pink-and-white stripes were turning a respectable tan.

We finished planting the south field by noon. I was mighty glad to see that job come to an end. After lunch, I jounced out to the new field in the back of the truck with everybody else, not knowing what we were going to do next, just feeling happy that I didn't have to spend the afternoon behind the stinking, roaring tractor.

In a neighboring field were rows and rows of tiny cabbage plants that had grown from seeds Manuel and the others had put in while I was still in school. Now those long rows of plants were up, and they had to be hoed and weeded by hand. I thought, *Weeding . . . hoeing . . . How bad can it be?*

An hour later I knew exactly how bad it could be. The crew spread out, each of us taking a row. The idea was to move down the row doing two things at once, thinning and weeding. Cabbage plants are set real close together to start with. Then you have to go back and thin them, so there's room for them to spread out and grow big.

It sounds simple but, believe me, it's not. While removing the extra cabbage plants, you're also uprooting any weeds that have begun to grow. You have to move down the row quickly, sizing up which cabbage plants to leave and which ones to hack down with your hoe, and at the same time attack the weeds. The idea is to leave behind the sturdiest, strongest-looking cabbage plants, eighteen inches apart, surrounded by nothing but freshly turned soil.

The others moved along in a group, working at about the same pace, except for Rafael, who was always slower than everybody else but me. Their rows looked perfect, almost as if machines had cultivated them, although there were no machines that could do this work. It had to be done by hand. And some people's hands, I quickly realized, were way more skilled at it than others'.

I watched Manuel from the corner of my eye. The motion of his hoe looked smooth and effortless. He talked and joked and laughed as he moved speedily down the row. When I tried to keep up the same pace, I found it difficult to control my hoe. The minute I stopped paying close attention or tried to hurry, I got all messed up. I'd take a wild swing and chop off everything, including the cabbage plant I meant to leave. Then I'd try to replant it, and when that didn't look as if it was going to work, I tried to hide the evidence by kicking dirt over the mangled body, which only made me fall farther behind. A couple times, I was sure I'd come close to chopping off my foot. Dad, or somebody, kept those hoes sharp.

After a while, I felt a fierce hatred for cabbage plants. I wished a plague of rootworms and beetles upon them all. I felt like whacking every plant on the planet. The only thing that kept me from trying was knowing that if Dad inspected the field, I'd be in for it. I didn't want Manuel to see my screwups, either. I didn't want him coming over to teach me his fabulous technique. I'd figure it out myself or die trying, which was starting to seem more likely.

My back was already killing me. Blisters were forming on my palms and fingers. Manuel and the rest of the group were at the end of the row, having a drink of water and laughing at something. I was less than halfway down my row. I did my own little inspection, looking back at what I'd done. It wasn't pretty.

I was tempted to throw the hoe to the ground and stomp away. But where would I go? Home, to explain to Mom and Dad that I couldn't hack it, after all? To a phone to report my parents' cruel and unfair treatment of me? I was fourteen. So what? So was Luisa. This wasn't even against the law.

I kept hoeing.

When the day finally ended, all I could think about was eating a ton of food at dinner and falling asleep in front of the television set, and that's exactly what I did.

8

As the week went by, my hoeing technique gradually improved, and what Mom would call my "attitude" improved, also. It wasn't quite so hard to get out of bed in the morning, my muscles ached a little less every day, and I was beginning to feel more like part of the crew.

It turned out that three of the guys, Carlos, Jorge, and Gilberto, were also some kind of cousins to Manuel. Antonio, the old guy, was Jorge's father. That made him an uncle to Manuel and Luisa, I figured. David was a friend of the family, and Frank and Rafael came from the same village back in Mexico.

They all spoke some English. Even if it wasn't perfect, it was way better than my Spanish, and it was enough so we could talk and even joke around a little.

On Thursday during the morning break, I was leaning against the rear wheel of the truck, sipping a cup of coffee. I liked the idea of taking a "coffee break." It sounded kind of cool, and it made me feel older, but I was still trying to figure out why everybody loved the stuff so much. The only way I could even pretend to like it was to disguise the taste as much as possible with lots of milk and sugar.

David slid down next to me on the ground with a sigh of contentment. He slurped from his own cup—black, no milk or sugar. Yuck. Watching him move so gracefully with just one arm, I decided to ask him to tell me the story. It made me feel kind of sick. He'd had an accident, the kind of thing that happened on farms all the time, the kind of thing Mom worried about every day.

Ten years before, he'd been loading a grain silo when his shirtsleeve got caught in the auger. Before anyone could turn the machine off, half his arm had been pulled in and cut off by the auger's blades.

When he finished the story, he crossed himself, saying, "*Gracias a Dios*, I was lucky."

I nearly choked on my coffee at that. "*Lucky?*" I repeated.

He shrugged. "What if there had been no one there to turn off the engine?"

I shook my head in admiration. I wanted to tell him I thought it was amazing that he was still working and that he was so cheerful and all, but I would have felt embarrassed. Instead, I made a joke. "You work twice as hard as Mula over there, and he's got two arms!"

David exploded with laughter at that, and hollered something in Spanish to Rafael. Making an exaggerated expression of surprised innocence, Rafael answered, but whatever he said was greeted by hoots and jeers from the rest of the crew. In the end, Rafael gave in and laughed, too.

I hoped he wouldn't take my joke seriously or hold it against me, and he didn't seem to. Later that afternoon, I heard him call, "Hey, Little Boss!" It took me a second to realize he meant me. He waved me over to where he was standing and pointed to a big garter snake in the grass. After that, I was Little Boss, and I felt proud to have a nickname, too, just like one of the guys.

I would have liked to talk more to Luisa, but every time I tried, Manuel noticed and glared at me until I stopped. Other than that, I guess he treated me okay. He was kind of formal and polite when he spoke to me. It was starting to bug me, because he kidded around with everyone else. Maybe he was being careful because I was the boss's son. Maybe he wasn't supposed to let *any* boys talk to Luisa. Maybe he just didn't like me. I wished I knew.

I found myself watching him out of the corner of my eye as we worked. It amazed me the way the crew listened to him and did what he said. With the exception of Luisa, they were all older than he was, but they seemed to accept his authority without any resentment, even Antonio, who was a lot older. I wondered how Manuel did it, but I couldn't put my finger on the secret.

Anyway, without question, the best part of the week was payday. When we got back to the barn that Friday afternoon, Dad and Uncle Bud were there working on the busted sprayer.

"Hey there, Joe!" Uncle Bud called when he saw me.

I was always glad to see Uncle Bud. His wide, sunburned face was usually lit up with a toothy grin, and today was no exception. Unlike Dad, who took farm work pretty seriously, Uncle Bud seemed to let the worries about market prices, ornery weather, and broken-down machinery roll right off his back. Dad was always saying farming was the best way for a man to make a living, and I knew he believed it. But Uncle Bud actually acted as if he got a big kick out of every little thing he did.

"Your father told me you were out with the crew," Uncle Bud said, standing up to greet me with a pat on the back. "How's it feel to be a working man?"

"Pretty good," I said, smiling back at him. "Especially since it's payday."

Uncle Bud whooped as if I'd said something hilarious. "You got that right, Joe," he said. Then he fake-whispered, "You think your daddy's gonna pay me for all my work on this sprayer?" He laughed again, in answer to his own question. With a wink in my direction, he added, "He doesn't know it yet, but he's helping me get in my hay tomorrow."

I grinned and nodded. That was the way it was. The uncles and Dad all helped one another out.

"Oh, by the way," Uncle Bud continued, "I left something in the house for you from your Aunt Kay. She said to tell you she's sorry we had to miss your birthday. I told her I didn't think you'd say no to a gift just because it was a little late in coming."

"Tell her thanks," I said. "And thanks to you, too."

Dad stood up then, taking a bunch of white envelopes out of his back pocket. He went out and handed them around to the crew, who were standing by the truck talking. I kind of hoped that when Dad gave me mine he'd clap his hand on my shoulder and say, *Nice work, son* or *Don't thank me. You earned it, Joe.*

Yeah, right.

Before I'd even taken the envelope from his hand, he'd

turned away to talk to Manuel about the trouble they were having with the sprayer. Of course, Manuel went right over as if he knew exactly what to do.

But even that couldn't ruin the pleasure of ripping open my first pay envelope and pulling out the check made out to Joseph O. Pedersen in the amount of two hundred seventy-eight dollars and thirty-nine cents! I couldn't stop staring at it. It was the most money I'd ever held in my hand in my life, and it was mine. I'd earned it. Right at that moment, I almost *could* imagine being the head of a household and supporting a family. I was a breadwinner, man! It was a very cool feeling.

I looked up to see Jorge watching me with a wide grin. "You win lottery, Little Boss?"

"Not exactly," I said, smiling back. "But payday—*es muy bueno!*" It was my first attempt at speaking any Spanish, and I hoped I was saying, "Payday is very good."

"*¡Sí, es excelente!*" he replied.

I had no trouble understanding—or agreeing with—that. He added something else, which I didn't catch. It made me wish I could communicate a little better. I remembered I'd had a Spanish dictionary back in third grade, and I decided to see if I could find it. It would be fun to sprinkle some Spanish words casually into my conversation while we were working. Maybe I could make Luisa smile. Maybe even Manuel. That would be something.

I followed the driveway toward the house, sneaking peeks in the envelope as I walked. Mom and the girls were in the kitchen, and they all gathered around to look at my check. Mom, of course, had already seen it: she'd written it. But she oohed and aahed along with Meg. LuAnn was way too cool to ooh and aah, but I could tell she was impressed and even a little envious.

There was another envelope on the counter with my name on the front. I recognized Aunt Kay's thin, back-slanted handwriting. Inside the card was a twenty-dollar bill.

Meg exclaimed, "Joe, you're rich!"

It almost felt true. But not rich enough for the Streaker, I reminded myself.

"I helped the crew to open up bank accounts, Joe, so they can save their money to take back to Mexico," Mom said. "Would you like me to do the same for you?"

I thought about it. I hated the idea of giving up the check and letting it disappear into a bank. What if they lost it or something? That was stupid, probably; everybody used banks. It was most likely the safest thing to do.

"Okay, Mom," I said. "Thanks."

She showed me how to endorse the check—sign my name—on the back, and write "for deposit only" so nobody could cash it before it went into my account. My account. I liked the sound of it.

Uncle Arnie must have shown up at the barn after I

left, because he and Uncle Bud and Dad all came through the door then. They stood around in the kitchen, talking and drinking beer, while Mom was fixing dinner.

Uncle Arnie was married to Dad's other sister, Mary. Mary and Kay looked so much alike they might have been twins, but Bud and Arnie were total opposites in the looks department. Where Bud was tall and red-faced and red-haired and kind of chubby, Arnie was small and wiry, with dark hair and deeply tanned skin. He was mostly a dairy farmer, instead of having crops, the way Dad and Bud did. He was quieter than Bud, but when he let loose with one of his loud, raucous laughs, you couldn't help but laugh along with him.

He wasn't laughing right then, though. Everybody looked pretty serious. I listened to find out why.

"I ran into Tom Matthews today," Arnie was saying. Mr. Matthews was another farmer, who lived maybe a mile or so down the road. "He needs more workers now that he bought up the old Dey farm, and he's applied to build some new housing."

Uncle Bud and Dad nodded, as if they knew about it, and Dad said, "I heard he's running into opposition from some of the neighbors."

Mom looked up. "I hope we don't have the kind of trouble we had after the Williamson incident," she said. "I'd hate for all that to get stirred up again."

"Me, too," Uncle Arnie agreed, "but Tom said the zoning board meeting got kind of ugly."

"What do you mean, ugly?" I asked.

Uncle Arnie hesitated, looking from me to Mom, as if he wasn't sure whether or not to continue.

Mom sighed and said, "Joe's working with the crew now. He might as well be aware of the kinds of things that go on."

"Well, Joe," said Uncle Arnie, "you know how people can be. Some of the neighbors showed up at the meeting to say they didn't want more housing for Mexicans—or any other migrants, for that matter—built around here."

"How come?"

Uncle Arnie shrugged and made a face. "They say it would bring down their property values."

I thought about that. It sounded stupid to me. Where were the workers supposed to live, in town somewhere? That didn't make any sense.

"It's pure nonsense," said Uncle Bud. "What they really mean is they just plain don't like having Mexicans around, but they can't stand up in a public meeting and say that."

"What happened in Williamson?" I asked. "I don't remember anything."

"Some drunken fool took a blind shot through the wall at a migrant camp and killed one of the workers in his sleep," Mom answered. "After that, for a couple weeks, there were incidents of harassment all over this area—fights, nasty letters to the editor, that kind of thing. It died down after a while. But our workers were very nervous that summer. Remember, Jim?"

Dad nodded, his expression grim.

Uncle Bud, always ready to look at the cheerful side of a situation, said, "Well, let's hope people have wised up a little since then."

I nodded. It was hard to picture something like that happening these days, especially in boring old Stanley, New York, where nothing *ever* happened.

Uncle Bud set down his empty beer bottle on the counter, thanked Mom, and said, "Well, I've got to be getting home. Kay'll have supper on the table."

Uncle Arnie said he had to leave, too. Then he said, "Oops. I almost forgot again." He went outside and returned with a wrapped present, which he handed to me with a sheepish expression. "Your Aunt Mary told me to give you this on your birthday, but somehow it never made it out of the truck."

I opened the long, thin box, which held a $20 gift certificate to the pizza parlor.

After Uncle Arnie had left, I went up to my room to wait until dinner was ready. I looked around for my Spanish dictionary and phrase book, and finally found it in a box under the bed. It was in with a set of miniature Peter Rabbit books, some G.I. Joes, a bunch of little plastic soldiers, and a stuffed kangaroo that I used to drag everywhere I went when I was little. It was a pretty weird combination of stuff.

I looked through the book. A lot of the words came

right back to me once I saw them written down with their meanings.

Buenas tardes, Señorita Luisa, I practiced. *¿Cómo está?*

Muy bien, gracias.

Mucho gusto en conocerle.

El gusto es mío.

I sighed. It was pretty formal-sounding Spanish. No one on the crew talked like that. I pictured myself going up to Luisa and saying, "I am very glad to know you" or "The pleasure is mine." She'd think I was nuts. The guys would probably fall out of the truck laughing.

I looked up something else. *Tu eres bonita. Tu eres muy bella.*

Forget it. I'd never in a million years be able to look a girl in the face and tell her she was pretty, no matter *what* language I used.

I imagined myself telling her not to worry, that I'd make sure no dumb rednecks would harass her or the crew while *I* was around, and had to laugh at how ridiculous it sounded.

To take my mind off Luisa, I counted my money in my head. Two hundred seventy-eight from my paycheck, plus the fifty bucks Mom and Dad gave me for my birthday, plus the twenty from Uncle Bud and Aunt Kay, minus ten for the movies and pizza, plus ten for my allowance equaled . . . three hundred forty-eight dollars!

Only seven hundred twenty-six to go.

9

That night I woke up to angry shouts and the honk-honk-honk of a car horn. The first word I could make out clearly sounded like, "Aliens!"

I sat up in bed thinking, *Aliens?* What the heck was going on? Had a flying saucer landed in the yard, or what? And who was doing all the yelling?

I checked the clock: One thirty-five in the morning.

Then I heard, "Hey, Pancho! This is America!" and "Go back to where you came from, beaners!" and some swear words, too.

I leapt to my feet and ran to the open window. I could see headlights from two cars that were moving in fast circles down at the end of our driveway, past the barns, right in front of where the crew lived. More shouts were accompanied by the crash of breaking glass and a rapid series of small explosions.

Lights went on in the trailers. Then one of the trailer doors opened and a lone figure appeared. It looked like Manuel. I heard him shouting something in Spanish.

Meg's frightened voice came from the hallway. "Mommy? Daddy? What's happening?"

I heard Dad's heavy footsteps on the stairs. Then our porch lights went on, illuminating the side yard, and I saw Dad running down the driveway toward the trailers and the crazily racing cars. I wanted to move, but I was riveted by the scene outside the window. And I was scared.

There were more shouts, more breaking glass, and then the cars began heading up the driveway back toward our house. I could hear the loose gravel flying from under the wheels. They were going so fast!

"Dad! Watch out!" I cried. I was vaguely aware of a terrible smell, like rotten eggs, filling the night air. Dad was standing in the middle of the driveway, facing the cars, and he wasn't moving, and they were speeding right toward him.

I screamed again, "Dad!" But he just stood where he was, right in their path. I didn't want to watch, but I couldn't look away, so I stood there, filled with dread and disbelief, until, at the very last second, when I was sure they were going to run him down, the cars veered around him onto the lawn and then back onto the driveway. Loud squeals came from their tires as they made the turn onto the paved road, and the engines roared as they zoomed away.

There followed a strange moment of quiet, and then Mom's voice came from the porch. "Jim, I'm calling the police."

I raced down the stairs. Meg was in the kitchen crying, and LuAnn was trying to comfort her while Mom was on the phone.

"Who were those guys?" I asked as I rushed into the room.

LuAnn shrugged, looking disgusted. "Jerks. Probably drunk."

"But what were they doing here?"

LuAnn gave me a fierce look, glanced at Meg, then back to me. Okay. Obviously, she didn't want to talk about it in front of Meg. I went out the door and ran down the driveway to where Dad and the crew were gathered outside the trailers. The rotten-egg smell was fading in the breeze but was still pretty awful. It had come, I realized, from some kind of stink bomb thrown by the guys in the cars.

As I got closer, I could see a mixture of fear and worry and anger on the faces of the crew. Luisa stood with her arms huddled around her chest, looking mostly scared. The guys were all gesturing excitedly and talking in both Spanish and English. Frank's face was grim and, I thought, frightened. Antonio and Rafael were scowling angrily, and Dad looked as mad as I'd ever seen him. He and Manuel were talking as I approached.

"You didn't happen to see any license plates, did you?" Dad asked.

Manuel shook his head. "No. But one was black pickup truck. Another was long blue car. Two men in the truck, maybe more in the car."

"You didn't know any of 'em, I suppose?"

Manuel shook his head and turned to the others. I assumed he was asking them if they recognized anyone. They all shook their heads, too.

Manuel leaned down to pick up one of the broken bottles.

"Leave that," Dad said sharply, adding, "I want the police to see everything."

While we were standing around waiting, Mom, Lu-Ann, and Meg came out of the house and joined us. Meg went up to Luisa and hugged her, and I saw the only smile of the evening flash briefly over Luisa's face. It disappeared as a police cruiser came up the drive and stopped near us. Two uniformed men got out, looked around, and began asking Dad questions.

"You're having some kind of disturbance here, sir?" asked the younger, shorter officer.

"We were," Dad answered. "It appears to be over for now."

"These migrant workers are yours?"

"These people work for us, yes," Dad corrected him.

"And where were they earlier this evening?"

Dad looked puzzled. "Right here. Why?"

The younger cop didn't answer, just asked another question. "They weren't down at the Bus Stop?"

The Bus Stop was a low-life bar and grill downtown.

Dad said somewhat impatiently, "I told you, they've been here all night. You ought to be asking about the idiots who came joyriding through here."

"So you know who they were, sir?"

Dad scowled. "I've a pretty good idea," he said. "It was

some of our so-called 'neighbors.' But they'd never admit it, the cowards. And I can't prove anything."

"Jim," said Mom, looking worried. She reached out to touch Dad's shoulder.

He turned to her. "Well, Vivian, I don't think it's a co-incidence that this happened right after the zoning board meeting, do you?"

Mom sighed and murmured, "No."

Dad said to the older, taller officer, "I'll bet if you talk to Tom Matthews—he's a farmer down the road—you'll find he had some visitors tonight, too."

"We'll check on that, sir. Now, why is it you think these neighbors of yours came here tonight?"

"To make a protest," Dad said. "To harass my crew. To try and scare them back to Mexico."

The older cop appeared to think about that for a minute before saying, "I'm just wondering why they would do that, unless your men provoked them in some way."

"Because they're ignorant jackasses!" Dad exploded. "Tom Matthews has applied to build more housing for his workers, and it's got the local rednecks all riled up. They say they want to protect their families from the likes of my crew. Well, what I want to know is, who's going to protect my family and my crew from *them*?"

Dad's face was flushed, and he glared back and forth at the policemen, waiting for an answer.

"So you're saying they don't like your men because they're Mexicans, sir?" the young cop asked.

Dad looked at him with exasperation, and I almost felt sorry for the guy. Dad took a deep breath and said in a low voice, "Well, officer, let me think. They came through here yelling ugly names like 'spic,' 'illegal alien,' 'greaser,' 'beaner'—let's see, what else?—'wetback.' Saying 'Go back where you came from' and making their point with cherry bombs, broken bottles, and stink bombs. Now you tell me, do *you* think they like Mexicans?"

"Jim," Mom murmured again.

"We had a report of some Mexicans being drunk and disorderly down on Exchange Street earlier, sir," said the older cop.

Dad spoke very slowly and softly then, which made his words even more forceful than before. "Well, now you have another report, officer, of a bunch of drunken, disorderly local men coming onto my property to harass decent, sober people who are minding their own business, trying to get a good night's sleep so they can get up in the morning and work harder than that trash ever worked in their miserable lives." He stopped to catch his breath, and I looked at the officers to see how they were reacting.

The younger cop flushed with embarrassment and looked down at his shoes. The older one, his face absolutely blank, took over, pulling out a notebook and pen and getting down to business. "So the vehicles were a pickup truck and a sedan, you say?"

Dad's expression grew a little less tight, and I felt myself relax some. Mom and the girls left while the questioning continued, but I stayed and listened, not wanting to miss a single word. Dad didn't say anything to me, but at least he didn't send me back to the house.

Long after the police left and I was back in my bed, my brain continued to whirl. I kept seeing Luisa's frightened face, hearing the crashing glass, and smelling the stink bomb, and trying to make sense of it.

I'd heard the word *spic* before. Randy had used it on the last day of school, I remembered uncomfortably. *Greaser*, too. *Wetback*, I knew, referred to the way some Mexicans swam across the Rio Grande River to get to America. *Beaners*, I guessed, was because of Mexicans liking to eat beans. And *aliens* meant foreigners. But why had those guys called our crew "illegal" aliens? Mom and Dad went strictly by the book. They wouldn't allow anything illegal to go on at the farm.

But I was beginning to realize there were a lot of things happening at the farm that I didn't understand.

10

When I walked down the driveway the next morning, I saw that the crew members were all outside, cleaning up the mess left by last night's joyriders. Watching them, I thought about how scary it had all seemed to me, even though I hadn't actually been the target of the attack. I tried to imagine what it must feel like to have that kind of meanness pointed right at you.

Manuel was raking gravel off the grass, where it had been tossed by the cars' wheels. David was holding a big trash bag in his good arm, and some of the other guys were tossing in broken bottles and the shells left behind from cherry bombs. "At least it wasn't the *migra*," he said.

Rafael, who wasn't doing much, just muttering and gesturing at the debris, nodded in agreement.

But Frank looked worried. "Yes," he said, "but something like this could call the attention of the *migra* to us."

Luisa was stooping down to pick up little pieces of glass, so I knelt down beside her to help. "What—or who—are the *migra*?" I asked.

Looking tired, Luisa shook her head and waved my question away.

I tried again. "Those guys who came here, they're a bunch of idiots," I said.

"Mmmm," she answered.

"Well, at least they're gone," I said, which was pretty stupid, but, as usual, I found myself tongue-tied around Luisa.

It wasn't only that she was a girl and pretty, and Manuel's cousin. For some reason, I felt like apologizing to her for what had happened, even though I wasn't one of the jerks who had come ripping through the yard the night before. I wanted her to know all gringos weren't the same, but how do you say a thing like that?

There was a silence that felt long to me. Then she said softly, "Maybe yes. But probably not."

Startled, I asked, "What?"

She looked at me then, and once again I had the odd feeling that she was older than I was. She seemed to be seeing past me to another time or place. Wherever or whenever it was, it made her eyes dark with sadness.

She stood up, brushed the hair from her face, and forced a weak smile. "I hope you are right, Joe."

I wanted to ask what she meant by that, but Dad came out then. He and Manuel talked a little bit about what had happened the night before. Dad said, "If those guys show up while you're working, or if anything odd happens, come right back here and tell me about it, okay? If anybody hassles you, ignore 'em and walk away. Don't get into it with them."

"We don't want no trouble, Señor Jim," said Manuel.

"We may not be able to avoid it," Dad said grimly. "I talked to Tom Matthews this morning, and our visitors stopped at his place last night, too."

Manuel nodded.

Dad straightened up then and turned businesslike. "Okay," he said, "so you'll be picking strawberries today, out in the far field."

"*Sí.*"

"When you've got a full load, bring 'em back here. I've got a truck coming to pick up the morning's haul, and Tip-Top wants a delivery later on this afternoon."

Dad started for the barn, but Manuel said, "Boss?"

Dad stopped and turned around. "Yes?"

"You pay like before, by the basket?"

"Oh, right. Yes. Same as last year. A dollar-eighty for an eight-quart basket. Sorry, I guess I'm a little distracted."

"Okay, good." Then Manuel cocked his head in my direction, his eyebrows lifted in a question. "Little Boss, same thing?"

Dad hesitated.

I didn't like the way they were talking about me as if I wasn't standing right in front of them. "What are you guys talking about?" I asked.

"Well, Joe," Dad explained, "the crew gets paid differently, depending on the job. For picking, we pay by the basket or the bag or whatever it is, instead of by the hour. With strawberries, how much you make depends on how many of those you fill up." He pointed to the back of the truck, where stacks of quart-sized square berry cartons were piled. "Eight of those to a basket."

"How come the pay's different for picking?" I asked.

"Strawberries have to be harvested just so. You've got to know which berries to pick and which to leave for another day, and you can't bruise 'em or squash 'em, and you've got to work fast. I need to get those strawberries to market when they're at their peak, or I take a beating. These guys get the job done. It works out well for them because the more they pick, the more they make. And it works for me because the berries come in quickly."

That made sense. "Okay," I said. "So why wouldn't I get paid the same way as everybody else?"

Dad hesitated again. Manuel looked away, and I thought I saw a little smile cross his face, which ticked me off. What was so darned funny?

"Manuel was probably thinking you might make out better if you stick to the hourly wage. Not being an experienced picker, you might make less than you're making by the hour. Right, Manuel?"

Manuel shrugged. "Is possible."

"Up to you, though," Dad said to me.

I didn't even have to think about it. Why should I slave away at minimum wage while everybody else made more? "I'll go by the basket," I said.

"Fair enough," said Dad. "Manuel will show you the ropes."

Oh, goody.

The mood was pretty subdued that morning as we rode out to the strawberry field. I missed the lighthearted, carefree fooling around I'd begun to share with the crew. But once we started picking, I forgot all about that.

First, Manuel asked Gilberto to "show me the ropes," as Dad had put it. I'd have preferred Luisa for a teacher, but there wasn't much chance of Manuel suggesting *that*. Gilberto was a really fast worker. He talked quickly, too, his gold teeth flashing, in a combination of Spanish and English. It was pretty hard to follow, so I concentrated on watching his hands and picking up what I could of his spoken instructions.

It didn't take me long to figure out that harvesting strawberries makes hoeing cabbage seem like a day at Disney World. At least when you're hoeing, you're more or less standing up straight. When you pick berries, you're crouched right down on your haunches, which is a *killer* position.

I couldn't believe it, but it didn't seem to bother Gilberto. He even had a way of scooting down the row in a crouch, without getting up at all. How his knees and thighs could take it, I'll never know. Just looking at him made mine scream with pain. He gave a quiet little groan whenever he had to rise to his feet, but other than that, he seemed not to notice that he was bent into a position that would cause most people to confess to crimes they'd never even thought about.

There were long rows of mounded dirt, with the plants surrounded by a thick bed of straw to keep the fruit dry and clean. Gilberto seemed to size up each plant in a quick glance, knowing which berries to pick and which to leave. I didn't quite get the distinction. They all looked pretty much the same to me, except for a few that were obviously still white. He began to hold up the ones he picked, showing me their even, red color. Gently, he turned over the ones he left behind, showing me that the underside was still pale and unripe. A few berries, the ones that were mushy or showed signs of having been munched on by some critter or another, he tossed into the dirt between the rows.

He showed me how high to fill each little carton before adding it to a basket that held eight cartons, or eight quarts. At the end of a row, I learned, you went back, picked up your full baskets, counted them, and put them in the truck, making a little mark next to your name on Manuel's clipboard to show how many you'd completed.

I can say right now that this was the worst day of my working career, maybe the worst day of my entire life up to that point. The pain involved in picking strawberries is simply excruciating, there's no other way to put it. Maybe someday I'd be able to scoot merrily along like Gilberto and the others, but I had a hard time picturing it.

When I couldn't stand crouching any longer, I'd try bending over and picking, until my back and the backs of my thighs hurt so much I'd have to search for a new position. It didn't take long to run out of positions. Every inch of every muscle, every tendon, and every bone in my body hurt.

The physical misery was bad enough, but the humiliation of my situation was worse. Now I understood why Dad—and everyone else—had thought I'd be better off sticking to my hourly wage. Compared with the rest of the crew, my pace was pathetic, and so was my haul. As the morning wore on, I watched the check marks next to their names pile up, while mine barely seemed to increase at all.

At a dollar eighty a basket, we were making . . . twenty-two and a half cents a quart. That couldn't be right. I did the math over in my head to make sure. *Man.* It didn't seem like nearly enough. I was beginning to think of each quart of berries as a small carton of gold. What did strawberries sell for in the supermarket, anyway? I had no idea. But in my opinion, judging by the labor involved in picking them, each quart ought to cost a small fortune.

When we broke for lunch, I multiplied one-eighty times the eight check marks next to my name and realized that I had worked five hours for less than fifteen dollars. I felt like a fool. If I'd stuck with my hourly wage, at least I'd have made twenty-five bucks and change. Luisa's sympathetic smile only made me feel like more of an idiot.

After lunch, Manuel and I ended up side by side at the beginning of adjacent rows. He began moving up his row at a fast, even pace, listening to his stupid headphones again. I saw that I was quickly going to be left in the dust. Joe the Tortoise, Manuel the Hare: Ha-ha-ha.

I decided there was no way *that* was going to happen. Ignoring the pain ripping through my legs and back, I crouched down and started picking like a madman. Okay, I might have grabbed some berries that weren't exactly ripe. Here and there, maybe a rotten one or two ended up in the carton. It's possible that some straw and a few leaves got tossed into the mix. But I caught up to Manuel about two-thirds of the way down the row and stayed neck and neck with him the rest of the way.

If he realized there was a competition going on, he gave no sign of it. He gathered his full baskets and carried them to the truck, and I raced to do the same.

That's the way the next two hours went. Then, as he had done halfway through the morning, Manuel left the field to drive the full baskets back to the barn. I was so relieved to see him go, I might have cried if I'd had the energy. The minute the truck was out of sight, I could feel every last ounce of strength leak out of my body, just as if a valve had been opened. I melted onto the ground and stayed there, unable to move.

I felt a shadow come between me and the sun, and looked up to see Carlos's tall form standing over me.

"You okay?" he asked.

I nodded and waved him away. Maybe I actually fell asleep, maybe I just lay there in a stupor. All I know is that by the time I heard the sound of the truck's engine and opened my eyes, it was too late. Manuel was back, and behind the big flatbed truck was a smaller pickup.

Dad's.

11

I scrambled to my feet, but the damage was done. There had been plenty of time for Dad to get a good look at me lying sprawled on the ground while the rest of the crew was picking away. When Dad got out of his truck and stood by the cab with his arms folded over his chest, I knew he was waiting to talk to me.

I was sure everyone was watching out of the corners of their eyes as I walked stiffly over to Dad. He reached into the truck and held something out to me. It was a quart of strawberries. Pale, unripe, dirty, packed in with bits of straw and leaves. I was surprised—and embarrassed—at how awful it looked.

I was dead.

"Is this your work?" he asked quietly. Somehow, when Dad got quiet, it was worse than if he yelled.

I shrugged, staring at the ground, too ashamed to speak.

"Look at me," he said impatiently.

I forced myself to meet his angry blue eyes.

"Is this your work?" he repeated.

"I guess so."

"You *guess* so?" He paused, and when I didn't respond he said, "Well, I *know* so. And you know how I know? Because none of these other people"—his free arm shot out to encompass the crew—"would dream of picking a quart of berries that looked like this."

I didn't say anything. What was there to say? I had really messed up this time.

"Well?"

I shrugged again. Wrong move. Dad was looking seriously mad now.

"Didn't anyone show you how to do the job right?" Dad asked, and you could tell he already knew the answer.

"Gilberto showed me," I said quietly.

Dad sighed. "Help me out here, Joe. I'm trying to understand why you would deliberately do a shoddy job."

Oh, man. At that moment I wished a big bird would swoop down and carry me away, even if it was a flesh-eating bird with hungry babies waiting. How could I explain to Dad, who always did everything perfectly, what it felt like to be the slowest and the worst, no matter how hard I tried? How could I explain to Dad, who always had himself under perfect control, that I did it because I got sick of Manuel always being better at everything than I was? Because I was jealous of the way Dad acted toward him, compared with the way he acted toward me. Because I got so mad I couldn't stop myself. How could I explain to Dad, who had worked hard almost every day of his life since he was a kid, that I hated picking strawberries and that I was so tired and sore and miserable I felt like sleeping for a month?

"Is it the money, Joe?" he asked. "Is that why you did this?"

"No," I said finally. "Not really." I had to pull myself together and think of some way to explain. "I mean, I see now what you meant about how I'd probably—well, definitely—make more by sticking with my hourly pay."

It suddenly struck me that Dad had been more than fair—generous, even—to give me a choice. The thought made me feel even worse.

"And I was pretty slow, you know?"

Dad nodded.

"I was working alongside Manuel, and . . ." My voice drifted off.

Dad finished for me. "And you were trying to keep up with him."

"Yeah."

"Joe, Manuel has years of experience working in berries."

"I know," I said miserably.

"So no one expects you to be as good as he is the first day."

"I know." *Especially you.*

"The most important thing is doing a good job, Joe. Cutting corners doesn't work. It always catches up with you. Someone has to sort through all those quarts you picked."

Before Dad could say it, I did. "I'll do it."

"Come on, get in," Dad said, climbing into the driver's seat of the truck. "The produce manager at Tip-Top is expecting those berries before five o'clock. You ought to be able to finish in time."

The ride back to the barn was a quiet one. It wasn't the easy, comfortable kind of quiet, either. Dad's silences always made me feel squirmy and fidgety. I couldn't help wondering what he was thinking about, and this time I was pretty sure I knew: he was thinking about me, and what a disappointing screwup I was.

I spent the rest of the afternoon re-sorting the berries I'd picked so Dad could run them into the local grocery store in time for people to buy them for their Saturday night desserts and Sunday breakfasts. When I'd finished and counted up the total, I discovered that my haul for the entire day had been reduced to a measly eleven eight-quart baskets, which meant I had busted my butt for a crummy $19.80.

I was disgusted, not with the money—or lack of it— but with myself. I'd acted like a big, fat fool in front of everybody, and I'd managed to accomplish the exact opposite of what I'd hoped for. I hadn't beaten Manuel, or impressed Dad, or proven anything except that I could act like a real jerk sometimes. I congratulated myself on my brilliant performance.

"Joe," Dad called to me as he started up the truck to leave for the store, "the berries in the west field are coming in fast. The crew is going to work tomorrow. It's up to you if you want to join them. After church, of course," he added as he pulled away.

Did I want to go back and face the crew and squat in the dirt picking strawberries on the one day of the week I planned to spend doing absolutely nothing?

No way.

Was I going to do it?

You bet I was.

12

I rode my bike out to join the crew around eleven o'clock the next morning, as soon as I'd changed out of my church clothes. On one of the narrow lanes I passed Manuel, who was driving the first truckload of berries in from the field. He gave me a wave and a nod. I couldn't read his expression, and I was glad to be able to start work without facing him directly. I planned to pick perfect quarts, no matter how long it took, and let that do the talking for me.

To my surprise, the rest of the crew hailed me as if nothing had happened the day before. They had to have noticed. I wondered if they were being kind by trying not to embarrass me, or if they were simply being careful because I was the boss's son. I wanted to think they were cutting me a break because they liked me, but it was impossible to know for sure.

Gilberto gave me a gold-rimmed smile. "Morning, Little Boss."

"Hot today, Joe." David fanned himself with his one hand.

"How about those Yankees last night, Joe?" asked Frank.

"They're looking good," I said. I felt my spirits lifting a little.

"Hi, Joe," said Luisa. "How are you today?"

I decided to try answering in Spanish. *"Muy bien, gracias."* I stopped, a foolish grin on my face, racking my brain for another phrase from my third-grade Spanish. Nothing came, so I pointed to her. "You?"

"Okay." She had smiled at my Spanish, but now a shadow passed over her face. Before I could ask anything, though, she smiled again and said, "Joe, when you're working *la fresa*,"—this, I knew, meant strawberries—"it is better not to look down the row. Keep your eyes on the ground. Understand?"

I nodded, not really sure I did know, but grateful for the advice, and for the kindness in her voice. "Thanks," I said.

We began picking. I kept my eyes strictly on the plant in front of me, resisting the temptation to look down the long row ahead. Luisa was right. By doing that, I was able to focus on the job at hand, and not feel overwhelmed and discouraged by all the berries still waiting ahead of me. I moved along slowly, ignoring the faster pace of the others, minding my own business.

When Gilberto announced that it was noon, I couldn't believe my ears. The time had actually passed pretty quickly. For once, I hadn't been painfully aware of every horrible second of every miserable minute.

It was noon, but Manuel was gone with the truck, and

I wondered how the crew was going to get back for lunch. Then I saw that Luisa and the others were heading toward the shade of some trees in the corner of the field, and she called for me to join them.

"Manuel is driving the berries someplace," she explained. "He knew he wouldn't be back, so we brought our food. You share with us?"

When I hesitated, she looked away and said hastily, "You probably want to ride your bike back home."

"No!" I said. "I don't. It's just that"—I held up my empty hands—"I don't have anything to contribute."

She smiled. "Don't worry. There's plenty."

Jorge had spread out a couple blankets and motioned for me to sit, so I did. He began unpacking coolers and passing around food, already munching as he worked. The tortillas I recognized. Then there were containers of beans, or, as Luisa said when she passed them, *frijoles*. I watched everybody else and did what they did, taking some beans, some chunks of meat, and some peppers, and folding them inside the tortillas.

The peppers were pretty hot, but once I got used to them, they tasted great. We washed everything down with paper cups of red Kool-Aid, which struck me as kind of funny. There we were sitting in a field of real strawberries, drinking strawberry-flavored sugar water. But, just like the food, it sure hit the spot.

The conversation was kind of slow as everyone tried, apparently for my sake, to speak English.

"Sorry, *no hablo español*," I apologized.

"No, no," Jorge protested. "Good for us. Good . . . *¿cómo se dice?* . . . practice!"

"For when the lady comes for English lessons," Gilberto explained.

"English lessons?" I said. "What lady?"

"Ginny. She comes on the Monday, Tuesday, Thursday. Teach English for us," David answered.

"You guys are all taking lessons?" I asked with surprise.

Everyone nodded, except Rafael, who shook his head. Pointing to himself, he said, *"Viejo."* Then he laughed and added, *"Perro viejo."*

The others laughed. After a minute, I did, too. I remembered *perro* meant "dog." I guess Rafael was calling himself an old dog, too old to learn new tricks. I figured that between being a lazy mule and an old dog, Rafael wasn't going to be studying English any time soon.

I was surprised that Luisa and Gilberto, whose English was pretty good, were taking lessons, too. They looked proud and happy about it. I struggled to understand. They worked all day in the fields and then took what sounded like summer school classes in the evenings? Were they crazy?

"It's good to know the English," said Frank. "Get to be better job. Bigger, more important, more money."

"Frank going be Big Boss someday," added Carlos, and everybody had another good laugh at that.

But Luisa turned to me and said seriously, "Most of these men never go to school, have to work. Me, I have to leave school, go to work. But I don't want to work like this all my life. In one school I go to in Texas, I learn about computers. I like that. In Yo Puedo I had drama class. We learn to say how we feel about things. I like it very much also."

"What's Yo Puedo?" I asked, trying hard to keep up.

"Yo Puedo. It means 'I Can.' It's a club we had at the school in Texas. For migrant kids. So we learn we can do many things, not just pick the fruit and plant the cabbage."

Then she looked embarrassed and said quickly, "We like to work for your father, Joe. He is good boss, not like some others. But is better, I think, to learn about other jobs."

I wanted to ask a lot more questions, but something she said really caught my attention. Dad was a good boss? Curious, I asked, "What are the other bosses like? The bad ones?"

She said something in rapid Spanish, and the guys snorted with laughter, rolled their eyes, and muttered comments I couldn't catch. But I didn't need to understand every word to see there was a world of stories in their expressions.

Luisa turned back to me. "Your father, he is a good man. He treats us fair, pays us fair, pays what he says he will pay. The houses here are nice. Clean, with inside bathrooms, not like some that have dirt and bugs, no furniture." She wrinkled her nose with distaste. "Your father acts to us with respect. Your mother, too. LuAnn, she brings *el café, los pasteles.* Meg, she comes, practices English with us. Is nice. Many people not like this. They look at us like, What are you doing here? You are nothing. But they don't know we save our money to help our family."

I nodded. It was the longest speech I'd ever heard Luisa make. I could see the emotion in her dark eyes as she spoke, and I felt vaguely ashamed. I hadn't had any idea before then about the other bosses, the bad ones. It made me mad to think of Luisa living in some dumpy place and being cheated and treated as if she were nothing. And I felt madder than ever about some of Randy's stupid comments and about the creeps who had come onto our farm on Friday night.

As we were putting away the lunch stuff, I overheard Gilberto saying something to David. I didn't understand it all, but I caught the word *periódico.*

I repeated it to Luisa. "*Periódico.* Isn't that the word for newspaper?" I felt quite proud of myself when she nodded.

But then that shadow passed over her face again and she said, "The last days, the *periódico* brings nothing but bad news."

"What bad news?" I asked. I hadn't been paying attention to world events lately, that was for sure. But I hadn't heard about anything big happening.

"Many people from my country died coming here," she said sadly. "These people, they came by the desert. The river crossing is dangerous, and other people have died coming over the mountains. So they thought the desert would be safe. But it was not safe."

"What happened to them?" I asked.

"The coyote—the man who promise to show them the way—he left them. They had no food, no water, very hot. He said he would come back, but he never did. Some lived, but many died." She was quiet for a moment, then added, "It is a terrible way to die."

I was almost afraid to ask. "Did you know them?"

"No," she said softly. "But I know others who died coming here. What Gilberto was saying before is that now Hector and his friends are afraid to come."

"Who's Hector?" I asked.

"Manuel promised your father to have more workers for the apples. Hector is one of them. He will bring others. But now I hope they do not even try to come."

I asked, "How did *you* come?"

She looked away. "Manuel, Gilberto, Carlos, Jorge, Antonio, and David, they came in the car. At the border crossing."

"But how about you and Rafael and Frank?"

Luisa frowned and hesitated, looking nervous. "We have papers," she said in a low voice.

Which didn't answer my question. I thought for a minute, not wanting to appear even more ignorant than I was. "You mean working papers?" I said.

She nodded.

"Well, yeah," I said. "You can't work without 'em, right?"

She nodded again.

"But what I was asking was," I persisted, "how did you guys"—I pointed toward Rafael and Frank, who were having a final drink of Kool-Aid—"get here? Plane?"

Luisa looked at me with disbelief. Then her face went closed and blank. "I think it is time to go back to work," she said flatly, and she turned and walked away.

I stood there feeling really confused. Up until that moment, I'd felt that Luisa and I were growing closer, becoming friends. But for the rest of the afternoon, she ignored me. Even though she was picking less than fifty feet away from me, I felt a world apart from her.

I kept thinking how different her life had been from mine, or from LuAnn's and Meg's. I thought about what it would be like to want to go to school, but not be able to because my family needed the money I could make by working. And how I'd feel, knowing that if I didn't go to school, I might have to spend the rest of my life picking strawberries.

And that I'd be lucky to pick for a good boss. Like my dad.

With all the thoughts going around in my head, the afternoon passed amazingly quickly.

13

That day, I'd hoped to ask my parents about some of the things Luisa and I had talked about, so I could figure out what I'd said that had made her turn away from me. But Mom brought up the subject of her family's big reunion again. It was less than two weeks away.

Mom's maiden name was Olmstead. She'd lived in Pennsylvania her whole life until she came to college in central New York. One night she had skated into my dad at the ice rink in town and, the way Mom told it, it was love at first sight. She and Dad got married, then we kids came along, and soon she didn't have much free time for visits back home to Pennsylvania.

The Olmsteads had a family reunion every July in Bucks County, where Mom was from. Olmsteads came from all over the country with their families and had a big old party that lasted for three days and was just about more fun than a person could stand. At least, that was how Mom remembered it, and how she described it to us.

Mom hadn't gone in seventeen years, and the rest of us had never gone. The middle of July was one of the busiest times of the year for a farmer, and Dad had always said there was no way he could up and leave to go to a party.

So we'd heard stories about the reunion from Mom, who got sort of a misty, longing look whenever she spoke about it. Being a good farm wife, she said she understood that the farm comes first. But this year marked the fiftieth Olmstead reunion, and Mom was putting her foot down.

"It's important for the children to know their own family. Why, some of my relatives have never even laid eyes on you all." She placed slices of meat loaf on plates and handed them around. "I figure we can leave as late as Thursday afternoon, stay Friday and Saturday, and head home Sunday."

To Dad she said matter-of-factly, "You've got the contracts all lined up for the rest of the strawberries. Manuel knows when and where to deliver them. The berries will be winding down by a week from Thursday, and there's absolutely nothing he and the crew can't handle for three days."

I could tell Mom was really serious about this, and Meg and LuAnn were looking eagerly at Dad. Dad chewed for a while before answering. "I know how much this means to you, Vivian," he said, "and I know you kids want to go. And you're right, the rest of the strawberry harvest should go pretty smoothly." He paused, looking troubled.

"But I'm concerned about leaving after what happened here and at Tom's place the other night."

"Do you think there's going to be more trouble?" Mom asked with a frown.

Dad shrugged. "No telling."

"It's so stupid," LuAnn said indignantly. "Why should people care if Mr. Matthews wants to build his workers a nice place to live?"

"They think treating them well will only bring more Mexicans to this area, and they don't want that," Mom explained with a sigh. "They don't actually know any of the Mexicans, mind you, but they have all sorts of wrong ideas about them." She shook her head. "It's so ridiculous, it makes me tired."

"I'd thought maybe things had settled down for good, until we had that disturbance the other night," Dad said.

I remembered what Mom had told me about the shooting in Williamson several years ago, and couldn't help thinking: what if the men who drove through the farm had had guns instead of fireworks and stink bombs?

No, I told myself. That was the old days. Stuff like that didn't happen anymore.

"Well, maybe this will all blow over," Dad replied. "I hope so. Meantime, I can't help feeling uncomfortable at the idea of leaving."

There was a silence while we all thought about this. I could see Mom fighting disappointment, and I could almost feel LuAnn and Meg hoping somebody would come up with a solution that would allow them to go, after all. And suddenly I had one.

"I could stay home," I said.

"Oh, Joe, no," Mom said immediately.

But I forged ahead as a plan grew in my mind, sounding better all the time. "I'd really like to keep the paychecks coming in so I can get the Streaker before the end of summer. And if I stay, I can keep an eye on things here. If anything weird happens, I could call the police. Or Uncle Arnie or Uncle Bud."

"Leave you home alone, Joe? I really don't think so," Mom said. But there was a note of doubt in her voice, and I could tell she was actually considering what I'd said. Dad appeared to be thinking about it, too. No one, at least, was voicing another outright no.

"It's not like I'd be totally by myself," I said. "Think about it. I mean, Uncle Bud and Uncle Arnie would come in a second if I needed help or advice or anything. This way, at least Meg and LuAnn could meet your relatives, Mom. And you could take photos of me to show everybody what a handsome son you have," I added with a grin.

LuAnn hooted and Mom smiled. "I'd like them to see you in person, sweetie," she said.

"This way's better, Mom, believe me," said LuAnn. "You can show them some normal kid's picture and say it's Joe."

I waved away her remark, not wanting to get sidetracked by a fight with LuAnn.

"I don't know . . ." Mom murmured.

"*Please*, Mom?" Meg begged. "*Please*, Dad?"

"It's only for three days," I said. "Nothing's going to happen." To Dad I said, "Anyway, we've got all this coming week and most of next to see if there's going to be any trouble. Maybe things really have settled down."

Mom was beginning to cave, I could tell. Dad gave me a long, searching look.

"Well, Joe," he said finally, "you seem eager to do this."

"Yes, sir. I am." I don't know where the "sir" came from, but it seemed appropriate for the situation.

"Do you really think you're up to it?" he asked, sounding doubtful.

"Yes, sir," I said emphatically. I relished the prospect of being not Little Boss but The Boss, at least for a couple days.

Dad and Mom exchanged one of those looks that meant they were going to talk it over without us kids around. They gave us the answer that's not really an answer: "We'll see."

Sometimes that's the best you can do.

14

The next morning I woke up to a chilly, drizzling rain. Strawberries don't wait for good weather, so I dragged myself down to breakfast. This time I heeded Mom's advice when she told me to take my rain slicker and rain pants and to dress warmly underneath.

"You can always peel down if you get hot," she said, "but there's nothing worse than being damp and cold all day long."

As we rode out to the field in the truck, I checked out what the rest of the crew were wearing. They had on layers of flannel shirts underneath their jackets, but nobody else had lightweight, waterproof gear like mine. Jorge and Carlos wore hooded sweatshirts, Frank wore his Yankees cap and jacket, and the other guys had on caps from farm machinery and feed stores. They had bandannas hanging down from under the caps to keep the rain off their necks. As we drove, Luisa took a plastic garbage bag out of her pocket, poked a hole for her head and two for her arms, and slipped it over her head.

"*Mejor*," I said, pretty sure it meant "better." I smiled, and watched her face closely to see if she was still upset with me.

She flung out her arms in a mock fashion-model pose. "The newest style," she said. "All the girls in Mexico wish for one of these."

I was relieved. She didn't seem mad. I wanted to offer to take the bag and let her wear my slicker, but I wasn't sure how to do it. Would she feel insulted? Would the guys tease me? Would Manuel scowl at me with disapproval? I chickened out, and just kept smiling at her.

It was pretty much of a drag, picking in the rain. For once, I was really glad to see LuAnn with the urn of hot coffee. It felt good to hold on to the cup and let the warmth seep into my cold, numb fingers. I actually drank two cups of the stuff to warm up my insides, as well.

After lunch, I came back out to the truck with two old, extra rain parkas we had hanging around the house. Luisa gratefully took one. Rafael fit into the other one.

Somewhere around four o'clock that afternoon I saw Manuel straighten up, shade his eyes with his hands, and gaze toward the county road that bordered our land about a half mile away. Something about his rigid posture made me look, too.

Peering through the misty rain, I saw two white vans with green stripes and some kind of official-looking insignia pulled up to the side of the road. I watched as four guys in uniforms got out of the vans, looked toward us, talked for a minute, and began heading our way across the field.

Silence fell as, one by one, each crew member stopped work to look and then froze. Someone asked a question in Spanish, and I heard panic in his voice. I could feel fear in the air. It was contagious.

"Who are those guys?" I asked. My voice sounded high and squeaky. I wanted to run, but didn't know why. There was nowhere to run to, anyway. The men were drawing closer. To my amazement, I saw that they had guns in holsters around their waists.

"Who *are* they?" I repeated urgently, when no one answered.

"*Migra . . .*" someone whispered.

Migra. I had heard that word before. I'd asked Luisa what it meant, but she hadn't answered.

"What's that?" I asked.

"I.N.S.," Manuel said at last. "Immigration and Naturalization Service."

Gilberto added in a hushed voice, "Border patrol."

Border patrol? What border? We were smack in the middle of New York State, for crying out loud.

"What do they want?"

"*Ellos,*" Gilberto replied. "Them." I looked in the direction in which he'd pointed. From the expression on the faces of Luisa, Frank, and Rafael, I knew who "them" was.

"Manuel," I said urgently, "what should we do?"

"Nothing," he said. "Just wait."

"Ginny heard that they were around," Luisa said despairingly. "But I prayed they would not come here."

Hearing the anguish in Luisa's voice, I had the bizarre thought that I had been set down in the middle of an old TV western, with the bad guys closing in on me and my unarmed companions.

But the border patrol weren't the bad guys, they were the law! And the law meant the good guys, right? I couldn't think straight, I felt so confused and scared. The tension seemed unbearable as we waited in silence for the men to get close enough to speak.

"Hello," one called out as they approached. He seemed to be the leader. His voice was calm and neutral sounding, but I noticed that the other three had their hands right on the grips of their pistols.

"I.N.S. officers," the man said. "Here to check your papers. Speak English, anybody?" Then his eyes landed on me. "Who are you?"

"Joe Pedersen," I managed to say. "My dad owns the farm. I'll go get him."

"No need, son," the man said. "This here's federal business. It's got nothing to do with you or your father."

What the heck did he mean, nothing to do with us? "But this is our farm," I protested.

"It's U.S. soil, and these people need papers to be here. So if you'll just step aside . . ."

Would Dad stand there and let these guys bully the crew? I didn't think so. "They've got papers," I said. Then I blurted, "Have you got a warrant?" It was what people always said on TV.

The man looked at me impatiently. "I don't need one. Now, listen, we've got a job to do, and we don't need you interfering." His hand was inching toward his holster.

I glanced at Manuel, who hardened his eyes and moved his head ever so slightly, as if to say, "Back off!"

I stepped aside.

To the crew the man said, "We need to see your papers." He spoke really loud, exaggerating every syllable, as if that would help them understand.

They're Mexican, not deaf or stupid, I thought sourly. It was obvious to me that the crew knew exactly what was happening. But the next thing he said seemed to take them by surprise. It sure surprised me.

"Listen up," the man said. "If your papers are good, get them out. If you've got fakes, don't even show them to me. I don't want to see them. And I don't want to see you again, either, *comprende?* I'm not going to arrest you today. But we'll be back. And anybody who's not legal had better be gone. You got a minute to think about it."

Luisa, Frank, and Rafael turned to Manuel, all speaking at once, concern and confusion creasing their faces.

Manuel looked just as bewildered as everybody else. There was a hurried, frantic discussion in Spanish. Then Manuel, Antonio, Carlos, Gilberto, David, and Jorge all stepped forward and lined up, reaching into their pockets. They removed papers from wallets or from plastic baggies, which they unwrapped and presented, one by one, to the officer. He stared intently at them for a long time, as if he had X-ray vision for spotting phonies, before handing them back.

The others—Luisa, Rafael, and Frank—stayed where they were, shuffling their feet and looking at the ground with frightened expressions on their faces. I was frightened, too. What was going to happen next? Had the I.N.S. officer told the truth? Or was this some kind of trick? Would he draw the gun now and arrest Luisa and the two men who hadn't shown papers?

I felt as if I should be *doing* something. But what? Could I stop the officers if they tried to arrest the crew? It didn't seem so. "This is federal business," the guy had said. I didn't know anything—except that I was in the middle of something way over my head.

After the officer had examined the six sets of papers, he handed them back, then spoke to the three people who hadn't moved. "We'll be coming around again. And, like I said, we better not find you here. You were lucky today. You won't be lucky again. Take my advice and go home."

With that, he turned and nodded to the three guys who'd come with him, and they all began walking back toward the road.

We watched the men's figures grow smaller and smaller. No one spoke until after they had climbed into the vans and disappeared.

Luisa broke the silence. "What do we do now?" Her voice was filled with despair, and I could see the trails of tears on her cheeks.

For once, Manuel didn't seem to know the answer. It was clear, though, that everyone was too freaked out to go back to work. "We go tell Señor Jim," Manuel said finally. Then softly he added, "But even the boss can't fix this."

We rode back to the barn in silence. When we got there, Dad and Uncle Bud were working on the engine of the big tractor. Dad looked up with concern as we climbed glumly out of the truck. He stood and came to meet us, Uncle Bud following right behind him.

"What's the matter?"

Manuel and I both started talking at once. Then we both stopped, each gesturing for the other to go on. Finally Luisa said, "The I.N.S., Señor Jim. They had guns!" before bursting into tears.

Manuel stepped over to place his arms around her heaving shoulders, so I began to explain. "They came right out in the field, Dad. I was going to come get you, but they said it wasn't any of our business! Then they said if people had legal papers, to take them out, so Manuel, Antonio, Carlos, Gilberto, David, and Jorge did. They said they didn't even want to see papers if they weren't legal, so—"

I faltered, not sure how much to say. I didn't want to get anyone in trouble. How much of all this stuff did Dad know about?

He was nodding, looking grim. I thought, *Uh oh. I wouldn't want to be in Luisa's shoes, or Rafael's or Frank's. Facing Señor Straight-as-an-Arrow Pedersen with illegal work papers.*

To my surprise Dad said, "They let you off with just a warning? That was lucky. They could have arrested you."

"They say they will come back," said Manuel. "And if they see these three, they will arrest them then."

Dad thought for a moment. "Manuel, I'm going to try to explain something. If I don't make myself clear, help me out." To Luisa, Frank, and Rafael, he said, "As far as I'm concerned, you always have work here. But I can't protect you from the border patrol. If they come back, you could be arrested, and there's nothing I can do to help you. I'd hate to see that happen. If you want to stay and hope they don't return, that's up to you. If you want to leave—go back home or go somewhere else—I understand. We'd hate to lose you, but we'll manage somehow."

I listened in amazement.

Uncle Bud spoke up then. "I heard that the other day a crew on the Davis farm saw a patrol van coming and hid in some heavy brush until they went away. Could be the feds are just trying to show their presence, make a statement, scare people into leaving, without having to make a lot of arrests." Then he shrugged. "But who knows? Some workers in Brockport got arrested the other day and taken to Buffalo."

Manuel translated this to the group, who listened gravely, still looking very scared.

Meanwhile, I was trying to take in the spectacle of my father and uncle talking openly about hiring illegal workers, or harboring criminals, or aiding fugitives, or *whatever* this was called. I was trying to comprehend that Luisa could have been arrested right in front of my eyes. I felt as if I had stepped into a world where everything was backward.

15

I was still in a daze when I walked into the kitchen after work. Automatically, I went to the refrigerator to get something to drink. There was a message on the notepad on the countertop saying that Randy had called. It seemed like ages since I'd talked to him. It had actually been the Sunday before, just eight days, but so much had been going on that it felt longer. After slugging down a glass of milk, I picked up the phone and dialed his number.

"What's up?" I said when he answered.

"José! Guess what? You're getting a day off from the salt mines."

"Oh yeah? Why is that?" I was still so distracted by what had happened that afternoon that I could barely think. I tried to push all that out of my mind.

"Friday's my birthday, man," Randy answered. "Dad said I can take you and Jason to Darien Lake for the day. He'll pay for all the rides and games and junk food we want."

It sounded great. Going would mean I'd be out a day's pay, but I couldn't miss my best friend's birthday, and going to Darien Lake was always a blast.

"We'll pick you up at eight Friday morning," Randy said, adding before he hung up, "and, dude, be sure to get me a really cool present."

Leave it to Randy, I thought. Okay, I'd be out a day's

pay *plus* the cost of Randy's present. But it would be worth it.

Dad had gone somewhere with Uncle Bud, so only Mom, Meg, LuAnn, and I were at the dinner table that night. I didn't want to talk about the I.N.S. guys and their guns in front of Meg, so I waited until we were finished and Mom and I were doing the dishes.

"Mom?" I said, sinking my hands into the warm, soapy water.

"Yes, honey?"

"Did Dad tell you what happened today?"

She sighed as she took a clean dish from my hand and dried it. "He didn't have time to go into all the details, but, yes. He said the I.N.S. came and threatened some of the crew, the ones whose papers aren't legitimate. You were right there when it happened, I gather."

I nodded. "But I don't get it, Mom. You and Dad knew Luisa and those guys had fake papers?"

"No," she said. "Not really."

I waited, still not getting it.

Mom sighed again, then gave a little laugh. "It's a very peculiar situation, Joe. I'll try to explain." She paused, seeming to gather her thoughts, then continued the circular motion of her dishcloth on the plate. "When Manuel arrived with the crew, we asked to see their papers. The law says we have to ask. They showed us papers. Now, your father and I had no way of knowing if the papers were genuine, but that's not our problem. In fact, the law also says we're not allowed to question the validity of the papers."

"That's weird. Why not?" I asked.

"To protect foreign workers from being harassed."

"But why would that be harassing them?"

"Well, all farmers aren't like your father, Joe. There are stories of bosses who find out about their workers' illegal status and use that knowledge to keep the crews in fear. They give them low wages and terrible living and working conditions—"

"Luisa told me she's worked in some really gross places like that," I interrupted.

Mom nodded. "She might have felt she had to put up with it because if she complained, her boss could have turned her in. That's what happens sometimes."

I scrubbed extra hard at the pie plate in the sink, thinking about somebody taking that kind of advantage of Luisa. I was glad there were laws to protect the workers from that stuff. But then I had another thought.

"Wait a second, Mom. It doesn't make sense. You said there are laws to protect workers from being harassed, right? So what were those guys doing in our field with guns? Isn't *that* harassment?"

Mom was putting some dishes away in the cupboard. When she turned toward me, she made a funny face. "That's what I meant when I said the situation is peculiar. There are laws to protect the workers from being treated cruelly. There are also laws saying that people who come here from other countries to work have to go through certain legal channels, or else they can be arrested and sent to jail or deported. That's where the I.N.S. comes in. They're supposed to keep people from crossing the border from Mexico—or anywhere else—illegally, and to find the ones who manage to do it and send them home."

I finally understood what Luisa hadn't wanted to tell me the other day. She and Frank and Rafael hadn't produced papers for the I.N.S., because their papers were fake. They hadn't crossed the border legally, the way Manuel had. They had sneaked across somehow.

I thought of the people she'd told me about, the ones who had died trying to cross the desert. I wondered how she had gotten here, and groaned as I remembered asking her if she and Frank and Rafael had flown over. As if she could have gone to an airport and jumped on a plane for the States. She must have thought I was making fun of her, or trying to pry information out of her. Or else that I was a real dope.

But didn't she know I'd never do anything to make trouble for her? Maybe it wasn't easy to trust people when you were an illegal alien, which I'd finally realized was exactly what Luisa was.

What I didn't understand was why it was such a big deal. I mean, who cared if Luisa came here and worked on our farm? Handing Mom the last dish and letting the water out of the sink, I said, "Why does the border patrol want to send them home? What harm are they doing?"

"If you're asking *my* opinion," said Mom, banging down a pot with a little too much force, "none. The truth is that farmers in this country, including us, couldn't survive without the labor of people like Manuel and the crew." She took the last pot from my hand, shaking her head. "It makes me so mad when people fuss about how the foreigners are taking American jobs. From our experience, that's just not true. We've tried running ads for local workers, and not one person has ever even called. Not one. Nobody around here is willing to do that kind of backbreaking labor for what they consider such low pay."

The dishes were done, but instead of running off the way I usually did, I wanted to stay and keep Mom talking. I'd never thought about all this stuff before, which kind of amazed me actually. But now that I knew Luisa and the rest of the crew, I wanted to understand what was going on.

I sat back down at my place at the kitchen table while Mom puttered around, wiping down the counters and setting up the coffeepot for the morning.

"Nobody wants to pay more for their food, Joe. The lawmakers and the politicians know that. They know the whole system relies on cheap labor. Which means foreign labor."

"Luisa thinks she makes good money," I said. "She says she couldn't make nearly so much in Mexico."

Mom nodded. "Our workers have always been thrilled

to have jobs. They're willing to take incredible risks to come here so they can work."

"Some of them die trying to get here," I said.

"I know. I just read about eighteen more people who died in the desert."

"It's like some sort of crazy game," I said, shaking my head. "One part of the government says they can't come here, and another part watches out for them once they're here, and another part arrests them sometimes and other times scares them to death but gives them a break—like today."

Mom laughed. "It *is* like a crazy game," she said. Then she frowned. "But games are supposed to be fun. And this one involves real people and their lives: the workers, obviously, and us, too."

I looked across the yard, past the barn to the trailers where the crew lived. I imagined them inside, huddled together, trying to decide whether three of them should leave or stay.

"What do you think they'll do?" I asked Mom. "Dad told them they could stay if they want to."

"I imagine they'll take a chance and stay, hoping the I.N.S. was bluffing. In a way, I hope they do. We need them, and I know they like it here. But, on the other hand, I'll feel terrible if any of them get arrested." She shrugged helplessly.

"What are we going to do if they leave?"

Mom gave a little snort. "We'll probably run another useless Help Wanted ad that no one will answer. And you and your father and the crew will work harder, and LuAnn and I will help, and maybe Meg, too. And we'll pray that Manuel has contact with some other workers who can get here quickly."

"What will *they* do if they leave?"

"They might actually go back to Mexico," Mom answered thoughtfully, then added, "but I doubt it. As I said, they risked a lot to get here in the first place. I understand the migrants in this area have quite a network among themselves. Our crew may hear of another farm that needs workers and go there. And if we're lucky, some of the workers from that farm will come here."

That really *was* crazy. It was like musical chairs. I was amazed by the weirdness of it all. Then I remembered something Uncle Bud had said. I asked Mom, "Why do you think the I.N.S. would bluff the way they did? If they *are* bluffing, that is."

"I'm not sure," Mom said slowly. "They must recognize how complex the situation is. I imagine they understand the futility of most of what they do. Maybe they're just trying to show that they're doing *something*. Maybe they figure word will spread that they're around, and a certain number of the illegal workers will get scared off without the hassle and expense of arresting them. I honestly don't know, Joe."

That's what it came down to. None of us really knew

what was going on. And how was the crew supposed to decide what to do when they had so little information?

Just then there was a knock at the kitchen door. I looked through the screen door and saw Manuel standing on the porch, along with Luisa, Frank, and Rafael. They must have come to a decision. As I jumped up to let them in, I realized that, like Mom, I didn't know what I hoped it would be.

We all mumbled greetings, but everyone knew this was not a social call. Manuel stepped to the side and motioned for Frank to come forward. Holding his Yankees cap in his hand, he nodded to Mom.

"Jim's not home," Mom said quietly. "You can tell me what you've decided, and I'll be sure to tell him as soon as he gets in."

Frank cleared his throat. "Señor Jim and you good bosses. Little Boss okay, too." He smiled faintly at me, waving his hand back and forth in a so-so manner, teasing me even now.

I smiled back, even though my heart was suddenly pounding.

Then Frank pointed to himself and the two others. "We stay. But"—he hesitated before saying haltingly—"we don't know how long . . . We are scared. One day . . ." He made a rapid motion with his hand, indicating, I thought, a need to run away quickly.

Mom held up her hand to stop him from saying more. Smiling warmly, she said, "Jim and I are very happy to have you stay. If a day comes when you feel you need to do something different, well, we'll understand that, too."

The two men and Luisa all nodded, their faces serious and grateful. I felt grateful, also, to hear that they were staying. Not just because we needed their labor, but because I realized how much I'd miss them if they went away.

But I was scared for them, too. That night, each time I closed my eyes and tried to sleep, I saw Luisa's terrified face, and the I.N.S. man's hand reaching for his pistol.

16

At breakfast the next morning, Mom and Dad talked about the crew's decision to stay. I didn't say too much, even when Mom said she thought that with everything going on they'd better not go to the Olmstead reunion.

"It's only Tuesday," said Dad. "We've got over a week to see how things go. I wouldn't rule out the trip yet, Viv."

Mom continued to look troubled, but I thought what Dad said made sense. And I thought it was nice of him to keep Mom's hopes up, since in his heart he'd probably just as soon stay home.

We were still picking strawberries. For the next couple days, everything at work was the same—and yet everything was different. There were the same endless rows of plants, the same aches and pains, the same sweat and heat and bugs. But we were all nervous and jittery. I noticed that the crew took turns keeping an eye on the main road, the farm lanes, and the hedgerows bordering the field. It reminded me of the way geese feeding in the fields had sentries on the alert, their heads up for danger. I felt myself looking over my shoulder and peering toward the road every few seconds, dreading the sight of those white vans with their official green insignias.

The fear and paranoia wore on my nerves, and I knew it had to be even worse for the crew, especially for the three who were in danger of being arrested. But the days passed without incident, and without any reports of raids or arrests or even warning visits from the *migra*.

Wednesday was the Fourth of July. We were working, and didn't do much to celebrate. But when it got dark, the crew joined us out on the lawn. From there, we could see the fireworks the American Legion shot off every year down at the lakefront.

I didn't care too much about fireworks, myself, so I spent most of the evening sneaking peeks at Luisa, who seemed to be having the time of her life. She was wearing the dress Meg had told me about, the one her mother had embroidered with flowers and birds. She looked great. She and Meg sat together on a blanket, their eyes wide with excitement, oohing and aahing over every burst. I wished I could go sit with them, but I was afraid LuAnn would make some comment to embarrass me.

At dinner on Thursday night, I realized Randy's party was the next day. I'd been so preoccupied when he'd called, I'd forgotten to even mention it to my parents.

"Dad?" I said as I passed him the spaghetti. "I know I should have mentioned this before, but I forgot. Randy's birthday is tomorrow, and he invited Jason and me to Darien Lake for the day. Do you think I could take off?" I hesitated, then added, "Or should I tell him I can't go?"

I made myself look right at Dad, even though I figured I was about to get a lecture about the importance of responsibility and planning ahead. To my surprise, Dad continued serving spaghetti without any change of expression. "Up to you, Joe," he said. "As far as I'm concerned, there's no reason you can't have a day off."

I couldn't believe it had been that easy. I'd had my arguments all ready, figuring I'd have to convince Dad that Randy's party was an important enough excuse to miss a day's work. But he was even smiling as he added, "I don't suppose it'll kill you to wait one more day to get that Streak of Lightning, will it?"

For a second, I didn't know what he was talking about. Then I realized he meant the Streaker. It was weird, but I hadn't even thought about the bike for days. "I guess not," I said.

I made a face, then said, "I'd be further along if I'd stuck with my hourly wage instead of going by the quart on the strawberries, though." It felt kind of good to admit it.

"Manuel says you're getting up to speed now," Dad said as he sprinkled cheese over his spaghetti. This remark, made so casually by Dad, stunned me. I probably shouldn't have been surprised that Manuel would report on my work, just as he probably did with the rest of the crew. But I felt ridiculously pleased that Manuel had noticed that I was improving. And that he had mentioned it to Dad. Maybe he didn't get as much enjoyment out of my screwups as I'd thought.

Okay, I had the day off. Now to the next tricky problem: getting a "really cool present" for Randy. Remembering how Dad had reacted before when I'd mentioned having Mom drive me around this summer, I turned to LuAnn and asked, "Lu, could you take me in to Wal-Mart after dinner? It'll only take a second. I've gotta get Randy a present."

LuAnn looked at Mom, who nodded that it was all right with her.

"Okay," said LuAnn.

I was suspicious immediately. I'd been counting on LuAnn, whose license was still new, to jump at the chance to drive *anywhere*. But, still, she had agreed, just like that, to do a favor for me? No deals, no bargains, no trades? A second later, I understood why.

"I wanted to go to town anyway, actually. I was talking to Luisa during the coffee break, and she mentioned that she'd like to go to the store sometime without Manuel so she could get him a present."

"For what?" I asked, feeling a little jealous at the idea.

"Just because he takes care of her and is nice," LuAnn answered. "Mom, is it okay if I go ask her if she wants to come with us?"

"Sure, honey," Mom answered.

LuAnn got up from the table.

"I'll go with you," I offered.

LuAnn gave me a funny look, but then she shrugged and started for the door, and I followed. I almost never went out back to visit the crew, the way LuAnn and Meg seemed to do when Mom let them. And sometimes, I guessed, when Mom didn't even know they were going. But I was eager to get a glimpse of where Luisa spent her time when she wasn't working.

There was another car parked in front of the trailers beside Manuel's old beat-up one. "Oh," said LuAnn, sounding disappointed. "Ginny's here."

Ginny, I remembered, was the woman who came and taught English to the crew.

"Luisa may not want to miss her lesson," LuAnn said, stepping up to one of the trailers and knocking. Manuel answered, and I noticed his smile for LuAnn was a lot warmer than any he'd ever directed at me.

"Sorry to interrupt, Manuel," said LuAnn. "Is Luisa here? I need to talk to her for just a second."

Manuel disappeared and Luisa came to the door. "Luisa," LuAnn whispered, "we're going to Wal-Mart. Do you want to come, or are you right in the middle of your lesson?"

Luisa glanced over her shoulder before answering, I guessed to make sure Manuel couldn't overhear. "I don't know when I will have another chance. I think I better come now, no?"

LuAnn nodded, happy, I suspected, to have company other than me.

I was happy, too. We all sat in the front seat of Mom's van on the way into town, Luisa in the middle, squeezed into my seat belt with me. Her leg was squished right next to mine, and her skin felt incredibly warm and soft. For a few minutes that was pretty much all I could think about. I was actually sitting right next to Luisa. Manuel wasn't anywhere near us. The only thing that would be better, I reflected, would be if *I* was at the wheel, making LuAnn unnecessary. But I wasn't really complaining.

I was so busy thinking these thoughts that I didn't notice how quiet Luisa was until LuAnn asked gently, "Luisa? Is anything wrong?"

"No," she said. I could tell there was more she wanted to say, but she seemed to be hesitating. Maybe she wasn't sure if she should speak up, or maybe she was choosing the right English words in her head.

LuAnn and I waited.

When Luisa spoke, it was in an eager burst. "When you ask me is anything wrong, I was at that minute thinking how there was *not* anything wrong."

LuAnn and I both nodded, not really knowing what she meant, and urged her to go on.

"Ever since the *migra* come, I am scared. At night I am afraid to sleep. I think they will come to the door—*crash!*—like I have heard before. But right now, in this truck, I am safe. The *migra* will not stop this truck to ask questions. So"—she shrugged and smiled, spreading her hands wide—"I am happy."

A lump had swelled in my throat when she mentioned her fear, but I swallowed it and smiled back. LuAnn smiled, too. It was impossible not to, when Luisa's whole face was flushed from happiness and from the effort of making herself understood.

Nobody spoke for a minute after that. Then LuAnn said, "So, what are you thinking of getting Manuel?"

"I don't know," Luisa answered. "I want it to be special, from me. Because he promised my father to watch out for me so much."

I'd never really thought about it that way before. Manuel annoyed me by always watching over Luisa like a mother hen. But it was good, really. She was fourteen and far away from home, and I was glad she had someone to protect her. I just wished he would realize he didn't need to protect her from *me*.

I tried to think of something special that she could give to him. "How about some new tapes?" I suggested. "He's always listening to those headphones. I bet he's sick of the same old music."

Luisa looked puzzled. Then her face cleared. "Oh, those tapes do not have music, Joe. They are lessons about—how do you say?—about your country, the Constitution, the laws. So he can pass the test and become a citizen someday."

"Oh," I said, feeling stupid again. And kind of small and mean. All this time I'd resented Manuel's headphones, thinking he was enjoying himself while I was suffering. And all the while he'd been studying.

"But, Joe!" Luisa said, brightening. "This is maybe a good idea, to get Manuel some music."

I felt a little better.

"Yes, this is good!" Luisa went on, giving me her brilliant smile. "You will help me to choose?"

"Sure," I said, although I had no idea what kind of music Manuel would like.

Then she said wistfully, "I would like to get something nice to send to my little sisters and my mama and papa, too."

"We can do that," said LuAnn enthusiastically. "They have lots of toys. And kids' clothes, too. I love those little bitty sneakers for babies. They're so cute."

"Yes," said Luisa. "I would like to see my sisters in those. But," she went on, shaking her head, "it is better to send the money orders instead. That is what they really need. Besides, Gilberto sent gifts back home to his family, and they never did get them."

"Why not?" I asked.

"They were stolen."

"Stolen? How?"

"At the border, at the post office, who knows?"

"That stinks," I said.

She shrugged as LuAnn pulled into the Wal-Mart parking lot. "Is what happens. People see a package from the U.S., they want it for themselves."

When we got inside, we headed straight to the music section. I didn't know what Manuel would like, but Randy was easy. His favorite group, the Toe Jammers, had a new CD out. I checked the price: $16.99. *Man.* I tried not to think of how many quarts of strawberries that came to.

Maybe Randy would like one of the CD's on sale, I thought. I checked them out. Pretty cheesy stuff. What Randy would call "orthodontist office music." I had to go for the Jammers or I'd never hear the end of it. I hoped he hadn't already gotten one of his parents to buy it for him.

Meanwhile, Luisa and LuAnn were looking at cassette tapes because Manuel didn't have a CD player. I joined them.

"What do you think, Joe?" Luisa asked. She pointed helplessly to the racks and racks filled with tapes. "There are so many . . ."

"What kind of stuff does he like?" I asked.

Luisa smiled and wiggled her shoulders a little. "*I* like music that makes you dance," she said. "But Manuel, I think, would want to know what *you* would buy."

Surprised, I repeated, "What *I* would buy?"

Luisa nodded.

"Why me?" I asked.

"Because you are, you know"—she smiled mischievously—"cool. All-American guy. This is what Manuel wants very much to be. Like you."

LuAnn laughed, then slapped her hand over her mouth. I could actually see the effort it took for her not to make some kind of sarcastic comment about *me* being cool. But it *was* astonishing. Manuel wanted to be like me?

I was trying to take it in when I saw two girls from school headed our way. I wasn't sure why, but I hoped they'd walk by without seeing us. I didn't feel like talking to them right then.

Too late. They'd spotted me.

"Hey, Joe!" Kelly called.

"Hi, José!" said Laura.

I winced. She'd obviously been talking to Randy.

"Having a good summer?" she asked. Before I could answer, she put her hand to her cheek and said, "Oh, I forgot. You've got to *work*." She made a pretend-sad face. "Poor baby."

"It's not bad," I said quickly. Trying to change the subject, I asked, "So, what have you guys been doing?"

They both looked bored. "Nothing much. Hanging at the pool," said Kelly. "Randy and Jason are there every day, too."

"I have to baby-sit the Blythe twins on Wednesdays," added Laura, making another face. "We should switch jobs someday, Joe. I bet you'd never make it through eight whole hours with those two."

Yeah, right, I thought, *and I'd like to see you make it through eight hours of strawberry picking.*

"So, what are you doing?" Kelly asked.

"Getting the Jammers CD for Randy for his birthday."

"Oh, I heard you guys were all going to Darien Lake," said Laura. She made a little pouty face. "I wish we could go. I'm sick of the pool."

She noticed LuAnn then, and everybody said hello, except for Luisa, who stood back, looking down at the floor. I watched as Laura and Kelly checked her out curiously, taking in everything they needed to know about Luisa in one long glance: dark skin, out-of-style clothes, old, torn flip-flops on her feet. Looking at Luisa, I could tell that she, too, had a good idea of what Laura and Kelly were thinking about her.

I felt suddenly furious. "Luisa," I said, "this is Laura, and this is Kelly, two girls from my school. This is Luisa," I added, wanting to make them acknowledge her.

"I am happy to meet you," Luisa said, smiling tentatively.

"Nice to meet you," murmured Kelly.

"Yeah," said Laura. "Hi."

There was an awkward silence. "Okay, well, see you around," I said finally, and Kelly and Laura walked away with a little wave. Their heads met as they whispered to each other, and their high giggles floated back to us as we stood in silence in the aisle.

"So," I said to Luisa, trying to pick up where we'd left off before, "do you really think Manuel would like something like the Toe Jammers?"

Luisa had that faraway look she got sometimes. "No," she said suddenly. "I want to get him a shirt. Pants, too. Like yours. So he looks right."

Oh, man. Luisa wasn't stupid: she knew Laura and Kelly had been sizing her up. I bet she knew that to them she looked uncool, foreign, inferior, poor—and she didn't want people looking at Manuel that way.

My fingers tightened on the CD in my hand, and I felt like smashing it. I wasn't about to tell Luisa that Mom didn't buy my clothes at Wal-Mart. My baggies came from a store at the mall where all the other kids shopped. Stuff there was kind of expensive. Mom ordered my polo shirts from a mail order catalog, because I was picky about the way the collars looked.

"Okay," I said. "Let's go see what they've got."

LuAnn more or less took over at that point, which was good, because she's much better at shopping than I am. She managed to find some shorts that looked as if they'd fit Manuel, and they were pretty cool looking, too. Luisa didn't have enough money for a shirt to go with them, but LuAnn assured her that Manuel already had some T-shirts that would look great with the shorts.

Luisa actually looked at me to see if I agreed. As if I was some big expert on fashion, or as if I'd ever paid attention to what Manuel was wearing, the way LuAnn obviously had. "Oh, sure," I said, nodding wisely. "Lu's right."

In the truck on the way home, Luisa clutched her bag as if it held treasure, and thanked us about a hundred times for helping her.

LuAnn even wrapped Randy's present for me that night. She handed it to me with a typical LuAnn remark. "Here. I've seen how you wrap stuff. No use wrecking a perfectly good gift."

"Thanks," I said.

Then she surprised me again. "That was nice what you did tonight," she said. "Just when I'm convinced you're totally clueless, you do something that makes me think there's hope for you."

She walked away, leaving me wondering if I'd just been complimented or not.

17

It felt strange to sleep in until seven-thirty the next morning. I'd almost forgotten the lazy feeling of lying in bed anticipating a day of nothing but fun and fooling around. For a minute I felt guilty, imagining the crew already at work in the strawberry field. But I shook it off, and thought instead about which rides I wanted to go on that day.

Darien Lake was a huge amusement park, with lots of great rides, including some wicked roller coasters and cool water slides and a wave pool. From the feel of the sun streaming in my window, I could tell it was going to be a perfect day. I jumped out of bed to get ready. Randy had said his father was going to pay for everything, but I stuck a ten-dollar bill from my allowance into the pocket of my shorts, just in case.

I was the last one to get picked up because I lived out in the country. Jason, Randy, his brother Tony, and Tony's date, a girl I'd never seen before named Shari, were in the bright red SUV Tony had gotten when he turned sixteen. I'd assumed that Randy's father was going to drive us to the park himself, and I was glad Mom wasn't outside when Tony drove up. There was no way she'd be happy about having me in the car with Tony driving.

Randy opened his presents in the first two minutes. As soon as he'd ripped through LuAnn's careful wrapping job, he handed the Toe Jammers CD to Tony, who put it in and cranked the volume really loud. Jason gave Randy a hand-held computer game. Randy announced that he already had it and tossed it back in the box, which struck me as pretty rude, even for Randy.

It was a two-hour ride to the park. It turned out that Jason had gotten a motorbike, too, sort of like the Thunderbird, only made by a different company. He and Randy went on and on about their bikes, bragging about whose was better and faster and all that.

I was feeling out of it, and I tried to think of some way to change the subject. "My parents are going away next weekend," I blurted. "LuAnn and Meg, too. I'll be home alone the whole time."

Now that I'd said it, I hoped it was true. But it did have the effect I'd wanted. Randy and Jason both looked interested.

"Cool," said Jason.

"Party time!" Randy crowed.

Tony and Shari laughed in the front seat.

"Spread the word," Randy went on. "Party at Pedersen's!"

Oh, man. Why had I opened my big mouth? I thought quickly and said, "Forget it. You know how my aunts and uncles are always coming around. We'd get busted, for sure."

Which was sort of the truth. One of my aunts or uncles really might stop by to see how I was doing, if they knew I was home alone. But I was trying to prove that I could take care of things without Dad around. I wasn't allowed to have kids over when no adults were there. The last thing I needed was to have Randy spread the word that there was a party at my house.

"Aw, come on, José," said Randy. "The danger of getting caught is part of the fun."

"Fun for you, maybe," I answered. "I'm the one who'd get grounded for life."

"No guts, no glory," said Randy.

"Fine," I said. "We'll wait until your mom is away sometime, and I'll spread the word."

Tony laughed and, to my relief, Randy and Jason did, too. A yellow Volkswagen went by and I saw my chance to change the subject again. I punched Randy's arm and yelled "Punch Bug!" at the top of my lungs.

That started a major brawl in the back seat. My dad wouldn't have put up with it, but Tony didn't seem to care what we did. He drove one-handed, with the other arm thrown over Shari's shoulders, while she snuggled close to his side.

I tried to imagine myself driving along, looking as casual as Tony, with Luisa by my side. Somehow, the picture didn't come together. I couldn't see myself being as cool as Tony, even when I was sixteen and could drive.

After we pulled into the huge parking lot and found a space, Tony thumbed through his wallet and handed a wad of cash to Randy. "That's from Dad," he said. "If you run out, don't come crying to me. Shari and I have big plans." He winked at Shari, and she smiled, took his arm, and drew him closer.

From the size of the roll of money, I didn't think there was much danger of running out. Randy's dad never seemed to have a shortage of cash.

Tony said to meet Shari and him back at the car at seven o'clock.

"Okay, Tony. Thanks!" I called as we ran off to the ticket booths.

Randy bought full-day passes for all of us, and we went through the turnstile trying to decide which ride to go on first.

"Definitely the Mind Eraser," said Randy, pointing upward to a new ride I'd never seen before. It was a huge, looping metal structure. At first I couldn't make sense of what I was seeing. I'd never seen a roller coaster like it before. The riders hung from a steel track in shoulder harnesses, with their legs dangling down. They rode up a steep slope, then came zooming down the other side and up again into a dizzying, full-circle spin. Their shrieks—either thrilled or terrified, it was impossible to tell—filled the air. I felt my mouth go dry.

"Come on! Let's go!" hollered Randy, running over to get in line.

I knew better than to wimp out in front of Randy. He'd never let me hear the end of it.

We staggered off the ride a few minutes later, and got right back in line to do it again . . . and again . . . and again. It was weird, but watching other people on it was much worse than being on it myself. It was fun-scary, not really scary. After our seventh ride, we moved on to the Boomerang, the Viper, the Predator, and the Skycoaster.

Then we went to the water park section. There were a

few girls our age there, and I couldn't help thinking about Luisa. I wondered how she would like being at the park, and realized I hadn't seen a Mexican-looking face all day long.

Duh, I told myself, *they're working*. Did they sometimes come to places like this on Sundays? I wondered. I remembered the wad of cash from Randy's dad, and I doubted it.

"Hey, José," Randy said, breaking into my thoughts. "Bet I can beat you at that."

He was pointing to a game booth where a guy was shooting a gun at some cutouts of ducks that kept "swimming" by, diving and ducking and flapping their wings to make it harder to hit them. There were prizes dangling from the ceiling, mostly stuffed animals of different sizes.

"We'll see about that," I answered. I would have liked to just play the game and try to win a prize, but with Randy everything was a competition. He usually won, too, and that's what happened this time. I was used to it, I guess.

Randy picked out a huge teddy bear. The girls we had seen at the water rides came walking by, and Randy went up to them and asked who wanted it. They all went crazy over it, and Randy joked around with them, finally giving it to the one he declared "the hottest." It was the kind of thing I'd heard Tony say.

Then Jason won a rabbit that was almost as big and gave it to one of the other girls. Randy kept forking over money from the wad, and we kept shooting until I won a prize, too. I picked out a giant panda bear. I held on to it, though.

"Oooh, isn't that cute? José wants a widdle beary for his vewwy own," Randy taunted.

"It's for Meg, lamebrain," I lied. It was for Luisa, but I wasn't about to tell Randy that. I had to lug the humongous thing around for the rest of the day, but if Luisa liked it, I figured it would be worth the hassle.

It was weird, but all day long—except for the moments when I was riding the Mind Eraser, which definitely lived up to its name—Luisa and Manuel and the rest of the crew kept popping into my thoughts. Everything I saw seemed to remind me of them and of my job: signs advertising strawberry shortcake, a game that offered Mexican sombreros for prizes, a tortilla stand, even a ride called the Hornet.

By the afternoon, I was surprised to find myself feeling bored and tired. Randy was getting on my nerves bigtime. For one thing, he couldn't stop calling me José, even after I told him three times to knock it off. And he kept on challenging Jason and me to stupid contests or wagers.

"Dare you to toss the rest of your snow cone into that woman's purse."

"Bet you're too chicken to swipe one of those prizes and run."

"How much you wanna bet I can ring the bell?"

Was it possible I'd never noticed what a pain he could

be? And how he was always showing off and making fun of other people?

"Look at that kid over there. What a load. I bet they don't let him on the ride 'cause he's too fat."

"Look at that loser in the checked pants."

"Quick, check out the toupee on that guy! Looks like something died on top of his head."

I remembered I used to laugh at the stuff Randy said and did, but that afternoon I couldn't imagine why I'd thought he was so funny. Jason didn't exactly join in with Randy, but he seemed to find him entertaining. I was actually relieved when Jason announced that it was a quarter to seven and we had to head for the parking lot.

We found Shari and Tony waiting in the car. Shari didn't look so hot, and Tony rolled his eyes and said she didn't feel well. She lay down on the front seat as we began driving down the thruway.

"Look at her, dead to the world," Tony said after a few minutes. "Girls can be such a drag sometimes. You know what I mean?" He imitated Shari, talking in a high voice. "The roller coasters are too scary, the other rides make me sick, I don't like shooting guns or throwing baseballs or darts, I don't want to get my hair wet . . ." He shook his head disgustedly. "I mean, why go to an amusement park?" Then he turned around and winked over his shoulder at us. "I met a hot chick at Jack's the other day. I'll take her next time."

It seemed like a crummy thing to say with Shari right

there in the car, even if she was asleep. I was leaning forward to look in the front seat and make sure her eyes were closed, when Tony pulled up beside a car in the right-hand lane. He was checking out the girl who was driving, giving her his movie-star grin and a little lift of his eyebrow. She smiled back. Then Tony gunned the engine, pulled past her, and sped ahead.

I closed my eyes, thinking I'd try to sleep myself until we got home. I guess I had started to nod off when I heard Tony swear and say, "Would you look at that?"

I struggled to sit up, and looked out the window where Tony was pointing. There was a car on the shoulder of the road, with the hood up and the engine smoking. Standing around it, looking bummed out, were seven Mexican-looking guys. One of them motioned for us to pull over, but it was a pretty halfhearted gesture. He didn't look very hopeful.

"Yeah, right," said Tony. He stepped even harder on the gas, muttering, "Drive a decent car or go back to Beanville."

Randy snickered.

"Hey, give them a break," I said. "Maybe they can't afford a better car. They're probably sending most of their money to their families back in Mexico."

"Or maybe as soon as they get a paycheck they go to a bar and blow it all," said Tony, with a knowing look in my direction.

There was a time, probably even that morning, when I

wouldn't have dreamed of contradicting Tony. I thought that everything he said was cool, and that he knew stuff because he was older. But what he was saying was stupid.

"Well, the guys who work for us aren't like that," I said.

"Oh, sorry, *José*," said Tony, frowning at me in the rearview mirror, looking anything but sorry. "I forgot those are your *amigos*." There was a moment of silence, then he added, "The thing I can't understand is why people like your father hire those guys, when they could give jobs to real Americans."

"Are you saying you want a job?" I asked.

He snorted. "What, picking beans? Are you kidding?"

"Well, you said Americans want those jobs. Like who?"

"Look, what I'm saying is they don't belong here. They don't even talk English. You know what I mean?"

How was I supposed to answer that? I shrugged and mumbled, "No, not really."

Randy poked me in the side and said, "Hey, lighten up, would you, José?"

I elbowed his arm away and said, "Yeah, well, you guys don't get it." Maybe there was a way to make them understand. "There are no good jobs in Mexico, in case you didn't know. They just want to make some money for their families, but people give them a hard time. Like the other night, some guys drove through the farm throwing stink bombs and yelling stuff like, well, like what Tony just said."

Randy laughed. "Whoa! That must have been wild!"

"So?" Tony asked. "What's your point?"

"So it was a lousy thing to do," I said, annoyed at the question. "It scared the crew. Meg was crying and everything. The police came. It was a big mess." I wasn't about to tell them I'd been scared, too.

"Nobody got hurt, right?" said Tony dismissively. "Somebody just wanted to make a statement."

"Freedom of speech, man," Randy declared. "It's a free country."

I couldn't help myself. "Lucky for you," I muttered. "You get to say any stupid thing you want."

Randy put his face right up to mine. "Oh, yeah? Well you know what, José? You're acting pretty freaking weird lately, if you ask me. Why don't you just move to Mexico or something?"

I ground my teeth together and tried to keep my mouth shut. What was I going to do, start a fistfight in the back of the car?

Jason said impatiently, "Can you guys talk about something else for a change?"

"Gladly," said Randy, sounding disgusted.

I kept my mouth shut and counted the telephone poles passing by. I just wanted to get home. For once, I was happy that I lived out of town, because it meant I'd be the first one dropped off.

It was nine-thirty when Tony finally pulled into our driveway. As I got out of the car with the panda bear in my arms, Randy said, "You and your beary sleep tight now, José."

"Yeah, right," I said tiredly. "Tell your dad thanks."

The downstairs was dark. My parents were already in bed reading. I stuck my head into their bedroom and said good night and headed for bed myself. My paycheck was on the pillow; Mom must have left it there for me. I looked at the amount and groaned: $176.78. Even though I'd worked on Sunday, I had taken today off, making it a six-day week. The first day of picking strawberries had been a disaster, and even though I'd gotten faster as the week went on, I hadn't come close to catching up with the others.

Rounding off in my head, I added $177 to my previous total of $348 and got $525. After deducting $16.99 plus tax for Randy's CD, I had $507 for two weeks' work. It was less than half of what I needed to buy the Streaker. Okay, so this was going to take longer than I had expected.

I lay in bed thinking about giving the panda bear to Luisa, and smiled.

18

When I came downstairs the next morning, Meg was sitting at the breakfast table with the giant panda bear on her lap, pretending to feed it Cocoa Puffs.

"He's so cute, Joe!" she said, her whole face glowing with pleasure. "Did you win him? I was thinking we should name him Jing-Ming-Ling."

Oh, man, I thought, groaning inwardly. Like a dope, I'd left the bear in the kitchen, and Meg had seen it and thought it was for her.

When I didn't say anything, she said, "Don't you get it? J for Joe, M for Meg, and L for LuAnn."

"It's a good name," I said carefully. "But maybe Luisa will want to call it something different." I hesitated, then came out with it. "I got it for her."

For a second, Meg looked so disappointed that I almost gave in and told her she could keep the bear. Then she said, "Oh," in a very small voice.

I tried to explain. "It's just that, well, you have tons of stuffed animals, Megs. And I bet Luisa doesn't have any." I poured myself a bowl of cereal, then looked at her to see how she was reacting.

Good old Meg. She'd always been a generous kid, more generous than I was, if I had to be honest about it. She was already smiling again, her disappointment forgotten. "I bet she'll really like it, Joe. I bet when she takes it home, her little sisters will love it! I bet they never saw anything so big! I bet it's bigger than they are!"

Relieved, I poured milk over my cereal and began eating. Meg chatted on. "Hey! She could still call it Jing-Ming-Ling! J for Joe, 'cause you won it for her, M for Manuel, and L for Luisa! Tell her when you give it to her, okay?"

Now that Meg had mentioned my actually giving the

bear to Luisa, I imagined myself walking out to meet the crew by the barn, holding a giant stuffed animal. I could already hear the teasing I'd get from the guys. They'd be kidding around, but I'd still feel dumb. And Manuel would probably give me that suspicious look that implied I was up to no good.

"Hey, Megs," I suggested. "Why don't you walk out with me and give it to her yourself? You can explain all about the name and everything."

"Okay," she agreed eagerly.

As Meg and I walked down the driveway toward the rest of the crew, I congratulated myself on my brilliant strategy. Everyone's face, even Manuel's, lifted in a grin at the sight of Meg struggling to walk with the giant bear in her arms. A burst of Spanish came from the group:

"Meg, *es tu amante?*"

"*¡Muy hermoso!*"

"*¿Pero un poquito gordo, no crees?*"

I gathered they were teasing Meg about her "boyfriend."

Meg walked right up to Luisa and handed her the bear. "It's for you. Joe won it. Do you like it? Do you think your sisters will like it? You could name it Jing-Ming-Ling. See, J is for Joe, M is for Manuel, and L is for you! And it sounds kind of Chinese, and panda bears are from China—"

Meg stopped, probably to catch her breath, and Luisa

said, "It's a good name, Meg. It's perfect." Then she looked at me and gave me a smile that took *my* breath away. "Thank you, Joe! Are you sure it is for me?"

"Yeah," I said. I wished the whole world wasn't there watching, because it made me feel really self-conscious, but it was terrific to see the happiness in Luisa's eyes and know I'd done something to put it there.

I dared to glance at Manuel, and was relieved to see that even he seemed to be getting a kick out of the big bear. Grinning, he took it from Luisa's arms and said, "Come on, *compadre grande, vámanos.*" He sat the bear in the front seat next to Gilberto, where it rode with us out to the field.

The crew was a little more relaxed that day than they had been during the week. As we rode along, they told me they'd gone to the big Tip-Top store the night before to do their grocery shopping. The way they explained it, a lot of the workers from the area farms met there on Friday nights, so they could visit and exchange news and gossip.

"No one has seen the patrol since Monday, when they come here," Carlos told me.

"It does not mean they won't be back," warned Gilberto as we climbed out of the truck.

"*Sí, sí*, we know," said Jorge. "We keep watch like before." Then he got a big grin on his face, reached into the front seat and grabbed the bear, and set it up on top of the truck's cab. "Señor Oso will watch, too," he said, cracking himself and the rest of us up. "He will scare the *migra* away!"

Whether it was because of Mr. Bear or not, the day passed with no sign of the I.N.S. Nothing out of the ordinary happened at all, except for Luisa's discovery of a tiny, spotted fawn huddled in one of the hedgerows.

I was picking away, lost in my own thoughts, when I looked up to see Luisa gazing at the ground and crooning softly, "*¿Dónde está tu madre, chiquilla?*"

I stood up with a groan and walked over. When she saw me coming, she motioned for me to go slowly. I crept up beside her, and at first I didn't see anything. She pointed, and after a moment I saw it, too. It was curled up on the ground, its spots causing it to blend in almost perfectly with the sun-dappled background of dead leaves. It opened its huge brown eyes in alarm, but remained frozen in place.

Luisa and I both began to back away as silently as possible so that we wouldn't frighten it into bolting. When we were far enough away to figure it would feel safe, we exchanged smiles, shaking our heads in wonder, the way you do when you see something that incredibly cool.

"I can't believe how small it was," I murmured.

"*Muy dulce,*" she said, which I was pretty sure meant sweet. "The eyes make me think of my little sisters back home." For a second her eyes glazed over with a mist of tears, but she quickly shook her head and pulled her baseball cap lower on her forehead.

"You miss them," I said, and she nodded.

I thought about Meg and LuAnn, and how they were always around. LuAnn mostly got on my nerves, and I guess I ignored Meg a lot of the time. But when I tried to imagine them being somewhere far away, along with both my parents, I could see how I might miss even LuAnn—a little, anyway, every once in a while.

However, I had no problem at all with the idea of their leaving for a few days to go to the family reunion. Better still was the idea of being home alone and being in charge of the farm.

Nobody had mentioned the trip in a while, and I was trying to think of a way to bring it up during dinner when Meg asked, "Hey, are we going to Pennsylvania, or what?" She looked expectantly from Mom to Dad. "You said you'd decide soon, and that was ages ago."

Mom laughed, probably because it had actually been less than a week since we'd talked about going to the reunion. I knew a few days could seem like ages, though, when you were really looking forward to something, the way Meg obviously was. I was eager myself to hear what Mom and Dad would say.

"True," agreed Dad. "I think we can plan on going this coming Thursday—"

"Yay!" Meg cheered.

Dad raised his eyebrows and finished his sentence. "Unless something happens between then and now."

"Things have been pretty quiet around here lately," I

said casually. "The crew's feeling better," I added, proud to be contributing something important to the conversation. "They met a bunch of their friends last night at Tip-Top, and nobody's seen the border patrol around. Nobody's been hassled by jerks like the ones who drove through here the other night, either."

"Well, that's good," said Mom. She turned to Dad and asked, "Speaking of that, Jim, what's going on with Tom Matthews's application to build more housing?"

"It's still under consideration," Dad answered. He frowned. "I think there's a zoning board meeting Thursday night, actually."

"That could stir things up again," Mom said worriedly.

I didn't want them to start dwelling on the possibility of trouble on the first night they'd be gone. Turning to Dad, I said, "If the weather stays like this, we should be finished with strawberries by Friday. I was noticing that the last cabbage fields we planted need weeding pretty bad. Is that what we should do next if we do finish the berries while you're gone?"

Dad looked surprised by my question, probably because it was the first time I'd ever expressed an opinion about what was going on at the farm.

"Well, as a matter of fact, Joe, I was thinking the same thing this afternoon. We'll have to get those fields cultivated, because the peppers and cucumbers are going to be ready soon. Once they start, it'll be nonstop for a while."

"And then the sweet corn'll be coming in," I said.

"That's right," said Dad. "Then we go straight into early apples."

"So this sounds like the perfect time for us to go on a trip," LuAnn pronounced slyly. "Mom, do you think my yellow sundress is okay to wear at the reunion?"

Mom and LuAnn began talking about what they needed to pack for the trip, which I thought was a good sign. It meant that Mom was seriously thinking they would go.

I turned back to Dad, hoping to continue our conversation. It was a new feeling, a good one, to be talking to him about the farmwork. I wanted to further impress him with the idea that he had no reason to be concerned; I could handle things while he was gone. But he was already excusing himself from the table, saying he needed to talk with Manuel about the next day's delivery schedule.

"What delivery?" I asked. "Tomorrow's Sunday."

"The Presbyterian Church is having their Strawberry Social tomorrow afternoon," Dad said. "Some of the crew are picking for it."

And with that, he was gone. Once again, I felt like an idiot. Nobody had told me about the church social or the extra Sunday hours. Maybe everyone forgot. I certainly wasn't going to beg.

Less than a week, I told myself, *until Dad leaves for the reunion and I'm in charge. Then things will be different.*

19

After church the next day, I found myself with free time on my hands. I thought about calling Randy, but decided I didn't feel like it. I wandered over to the window and was surprised to see LuAnn, Meg, and Luisa sitting on chaise lounges under the big maple tree in our yard, drinking lemonade, talking, and laughing. I watched for a minute, then went outside to join them.

"Hi, Joe!" called Meg, giving me a big wave.

Luisa, too, said hi, as I wandered over in what I hoped was a casual manner, pulled up a chair, and sat down.

"I thought everybody was working," I said to Luisa.

"The others are," she said. "But I had laundry and cooking to do. I am making a special dinner for everyone tonight. And tonight I will give Manuel the pants, the baggies."

"Luisa showed them to me," Meg said proudly. "Manuel's going to like them, don't you think?"

"I know he will," said Luisa happily.

"So, Joe," LuAnn said, "if everybody else is working, how come you're not?"

I shrugged. "I had stuff to do, too," I said vaguely.

Luckily, she didn't ask me what. Instead, she turned to Luisa and said, "Joe's saving up to buy a motorbike."

Luisa looked puzzled.

"You know motorcycles, right?" LuAnn asked. "Two wheels, fast, loud?"

Luisa nodded.

"Well, it's sort of like a toy one of those, for kids who can't drive yet. He won't be able to ride it on the road or anything, just in the fields and along railroad beds and places like that."

Oh, man. I groaned inwardly. *Thanks a lot, LuAnn. Make me sound like a total dork, why don't you?*

Luisa was looking at me now, her puzzled expression back. "Why do you want this, Joe?" she asked.

"I—Well—" I stopped, trying to think what to say. Right then, I couldn't remember exactly why I did want the Streaker so much. But that wasn't the only reason I felt tongue-tied. I mean, here was Luisa, working so she could send money home to her family, money for food and clothes and stuff like that. I felt like a real jerk working so I could buy what LuAnn had just described as a *toy*.

Meg chimed in then, saying, "So he can take me for rides! Right, Joe?"

"Right," I mumbled, looking at Luisa and shrugging, as if to say, "You know how it is with little sisters." As if taking Meg for rides was my only reason for wanting the bike. Joe the magnanimous big brother, that's me.

LuAnn must have been feeling merciful, or else she was tired of the subject, because she didn't pursue it any further. Thank goodness.

As Luisa and LuAnn talked about what Luisa was

cooking, I imagined her turning to me and saying, "Joe, would you like to come and join us for the special supper I am making?"

But I knew she wouldn't. I thought about inviting myself and offering to bring something, the way we did with my aunts and uncles, and they did with us. But I knew I wouldn't. I wasn't part of Luisa's family and, even though I was feeling more like part of the crew all the time, I'd always be the boss's son. I'd definitely have liked to spend an evening with Luisa, but I was way too chicken to risk saying so.

I told myself to forget the whole idea. If I didn't ask, she couldn't say no. That was playing it safe. Then I thought, *If you keep playing it safe, nothing will ever happen.*

The more I thought about it, the more complicated it got. Lately, *everything* seemed complicated. Maybe it always had been, and I'd never noticed before.

20

For the next three days, I thought Mom was going to drive us—and herself—crazy. She couldn't stop fussing about the reunion trip. It had been her idea, but as the time grew closer she started talking about backing out.

"I'm just not sure we should go," she'd say about a

hundred times a day. "I can't help worrying about leaving Joe. I keep thinking of all the things that could happen . . ."

One minute she'd be talking about what she was going to pack, the next minute she'd say, "We shouldn't go. We'll just stay home." Or she'd say, "Don't forget to put the trash out on Friday morning," or, "You have to watch this burner on the stove; it doesn't always light." Then she'd get a frazzled look on her face, throw up her hands, and say, "Never mind. We're not going anywhere."

I had to hand it to Dad. It would have been easy to say, "Okay, we'll stay home." Especially since that's what he probably wanted to do. But he knew Mom. And I guess he knew that she really wanted to go, even though she couldn't help worrying. He kept telling her everything was going to be fine, and he went right ahead looking at road maps to plan the route they'd take.

I believed he really *wasn't* worried, and that made me feel pretty good. If Dad wasn't concerned, it meant he had confidence in me. It meant he knew I could take care of things while they were gone. But Wednesday night when I was mowing the side yard after dinner, Dad came out and signaled for me to cut the engine so we could talk.

"Joe, you know how much this trip to Pennsylvania means to your mother," he began.

I nodded.

"But I'm afraid she's going to be fretting about you the whole time we're gone."

I smiled and shrugged. "She'll see. I'll be fine."

"Well, I've been thinking," Dad went on. "I understand that you don't want to come along because you'd miss three days' pay toward that motorbike. But I know your mother would feel a lot better about leaving—and I would, too—if you stayed with Aunt Kay or Aunt Mary. They've both offered to have you. Your cousins would love it."

My cousins were great, but they were a lot younger than I was. When they weren't climbing on me as if I was a piece of playground equipment, they were saying, "Joe, what are we gonna do now? Huh, Joe?" They were okay in small doses, but they wore me out fast.

"I know, Dad," I said quickly, "but somebody's got to keep an eye on things around here."

"I've talked to Manuel about that," Dad said. "He's all set. It's you we're concerned about."

I couldn't believe it. He didn't even think I could take care of myself, not to mention the farm. I'd been kidding myself thinking he was leaving me in charge. Joe the Big Boss? What a joke.

For a minute, I was too stunned and mad to speak. What did he think—I needed one of my aunts to cook my meals and tuck me into bed? Manuel could be head of a household and Luisa could work to support her family, but I was so pathetic I needed a baby-sitter because my mommy was going away for three days?

The air smelled strongly of freshly mown grass, and I

took a deep breath. If I lost it and said what I was thinking, it would just make him mad. He'd probably tell me to go to my room, as if I were still a kid. I had to stay cool.

When I thought I could control my voice, I said, "Dad, Mom's going to worry no matter where I stay, you know that. It'll be so much easier for everybody if I just stay here. Nobody'll have to drop me off and pick me up for work and all that. Besides, I think it's important for somebody to be here. Somebody from the family," I emphasized.

Dad appeared to be listening. At least he wasn't arguing.

"I want to prove you can trust me and that I care about the farm, too, but how can I do it if you don't give me a chance?" I asked.

Dad was quiet for a minute. Then he nodded. "All right, Joe. You've got your chance. You finish the lawn, and I'll go tell your mother."

21

When I came home at lunchtime the next day, Mom's van was all packed. While I ate, she went over the lists she'd written for me: lists of phone numbers and things to do and things to be sure and remember *not* to do. I nodded and listened patiently, not wanting to give her any reason to change her mind at the last second.

As usual, the lunch hour passed quickly, and soon it was time for me to go back to work. I got up from the table and said goodbye to everybody, because the plan was for them to leave around three o'clock, and I wouldn't see them again until Sunday.

"Have a great trip, and *don't worry*, okay?" I said.

Meg threw her arms around me and gave me a good-bye kiss.

LuAnn gave me an evil grin and said, "Try not to do anything too stupid."

Dad gave me a hug and Mom kissed me a whole bunch of times, and I left in a flurry of "goodbyes" and "be carefuls" and other last-minute instructions.

When I came back to the house after work, they were actually gone. I was enjoying the feeling of having the place all to myself when the phone rang. It was Aunt Kay.

"Are you sure you're okay there by yourself, Joe?" she asked.

"Couldn't be better," I assured her.

"You know you're welcome to sleep over here tonight. Your Uncle Bud can come get you and drive you home in the morning."

"I know. Thanks. But I'm okay, really."

"Well, then, how about having supper with us to-night?"

"Thanks, Aunt Kay, really, but I've got stuff to do." This wasn't exactly true, but nobody seemed to get it: I wouldn't be on my own if I simply let Uncle Bud and Aunt Kay take over for Mom and Dad.

"Did your folks get in safe?" she asked.

"They said they'd call from Grandma Olmstead's house, but they won't get there for"—I glanced at the clock—"another two and a half hours or so."

"Okay, well, listen, when you talk to them, tell them the zoning board meeting was cancelled for tonight because so many board members are away on vacation. I know your mom was worried that a yes vote about Tom Matthews's project might stir up more trouble like you had before. This'll help set her mind at ease so she'll be able to enjoy herself."

"Okay," I said. "I'll be sure to tell her." This news set my mind at ease, too. I didn't have to worry about those guys coming back for another late-night drive through the farm.

"You call now, if you need anything, you hear?" Aunt Kay instructed.

"I will. Thanks."

"Your Uncle Bud'll be over tomorrow to see how you're doing."

"Okay, great. Thanks. 'Bye."

As soon as I hung up the phone, it rang again, and I went through practically the same conversation with Aunt Mary. I warmed up the macaroni and cheese Mom had left me and took it outside on the porch to eat before the phone could ring again.

Later, when I was doing my dishes, Aunt Kay called back "just to check," and my parents called to say they'd arrived safely. After that I felt like leaving the phone off the hook. But, knowing my relatives, one of them would probably drive over to make sure nothing was wrong.

I watched a little TV and turned in early, the way I'd been doing all summer. But I didn't get much sleep. It wasn't that I was scared of being alone in the house or anything like that. The thing was, I was used to Mom sticking her head in my room to wake me up in the morning. With her gone, I was so worried about oversleeping that I could hardly get to sleep at all. I kept sitting up in bed and turning on the light to check the alarm clock. Had I set it right? Had I moved the little switch to ON? Had I mistakenly set it for six p.m. instead of a.m.?

I was relieved when the stupid thing finally rang and it was time to get up.

I went out to the truck, where the crew had already started to gather. Everyone was there except for Manuel and Carlos. As I walked closer, Frank made a big show of pretending to look scared. "¡Silencio, todos!" he said in a loud whisper. "Quiet, everyone. No fooling around. The Big Boss is here!"

The others straightened up and tried to look serious, but they couldn't hide their grins as David swept off his hat and gave me a humble bow.

"Morning, Boss," he said. "We are—how you say?—*at your service.*"

Everybody cracked up at that.

"At my service, eh? Well, then, you can—" I was about to kid him back and say something kind of crude, when I remembered that Luisa was there. "Never mind."

"Whatever you say, Boss," Jorge said, giving me a sly wink.

"Hey, Boss," said Rafael. "We finish *la fresa* today, we take the rest of the day off, *sí*?"

"*No problema, Mula,*" I said. "You take off all the time you want." I paused and added, "Just remind me to take off dollars from your paycheck."

Everybody was laughing and hooting at Rafael as Manuel and Carlos came out of one of the trailers and joined us. Manuel said good morning to everyone. When he jumped into the truck, the rest of us followed, taking our places in the rear bed. It just went to prove what I knew deep inside. There wasn't really any question about who was the boss.

As it turned out, we did finish the strawberries that afternoon. Manuel drove off with the final load, and I got to play the part of Big Boss for a couple minutes, handing out the Friday night paychecks. Since Mom knew she was going to be away, she estimated each person's haul for Thursday and Friday. My check was up to a respectable $249.38. I'd improved at berry picking, but hadn't reached the point at which I made as much as I would on an hourly wage. So I was actually glad we were going back to hoeing cabbage. I hadn't forgotten how hard and boring it was, but at least I'd get paid by the hour.

Uncle Bud drove in around six-thirty to see how things were going, and to bring me some cookies Aunt Kay had made. He said she'd told him to ask me again to come to supper. Before I had a chance to answer, Aunt Mary pulled up with a basket full of fried chicken, rolls, potato salad, and baked beans.

"Couldn't let my favorite nephew go hungry," she said, handing me the food with a smile.

I couldn't help laughing. Why fight it? After one whiff of that fried chicken, all my big ideas about taking care of myself and being totally on my own flew right out of my head. I thanked Aunt Mary and Uncle Bud, and went inside to chow down.

After dinner I tried to watch TV, but the summer reruns stunk, and I felt too restless to sit inside. It was starting to get dark, but I decided to go out. I had told Dad someone from the family should be here to keep an eye on things, so I figured I ought to take a look around the barns and the yard. I didn't know what I was looking for—anything that seemed amiss, I guess. Maybe I'd discover an intruder or something, and get my chance to be a big hero. Yeah, right.

I found myself drawing closer and closer to the crew's quarters, and realized that part of what had drawn me outside was the hope of catching a glimpse of Luisa. Behind her trailer, the last pinkish-orange glow of the sunset was fading away. I stood very still, watching the shadows steal across the fields, letting the moist, heavy quiet of the summer night wrap around me like a blanket. Below our farm, to the east, lights came on in the cottages surrounding Seneca Lake, making its waters appear deep and dark and mysterious.

Maybe it was because I was feeling responsible for watching over the place, maybe it was because the air was so sweet and rich with the smell of growing things, or because the familiar chirps of the crickets and tree frogs and birds sounded so peaceful. For some reason, I felt I was really seeing our farm for the first time in a long while. I'd so often wished I lived in town that I hadn't paid attention to the beauty of the land and the sky and the water all about me.

There had been so many things on my mind lately, and in my heart, too, and they seemed to rise up in the middle of my chest. I felt an ache there, as if there wasn't room for all those feelings at once.

A voice spoke softly. "It is very beautiful, no?"

At first I wasn't sure if I'd heard words or the echo of my own thoughts.

Then I became aware of a shape in the shadows beneath the big maple tree, and my heart made a strange leap.

"Luisa?"

"Hi, Joe."

"Hi." I walked closer. She was sitting alone under the tree. She must have been there the whole time. "I was— just looking around."

"Yes, I saw you."

Maybe it was the gathering darkness that gave me the courage to ask, "Okay if I sit down?"

"Sure."

I sat on the ground beside her, leaning my back against the tree trunk. "What are you doing?"

"I come here most nights."

"Really? What for?"

She pointed toward the sky. "I watch the sun go away. I look up, I watch *las estrellas*—the stars—come out. I wait for the moon to rise."

I, too, gazed upward. Even as I watched, more stars appeared.

"When I left Mexico," Luisa continued quietly, "my mother told me, 'When you are lonely, when it seems you will never see us again, look up to the sky.' She said, 'Remember, Luisa, that we are under the same sky—the same sun, the same moon, the same stars. We are watching, too.' "

I gazed at the sky, imagining Luisa's sisters, and her mother and father, looking up into the heavens at that very moment.

"When I do this," Luisa said, "they do not seem so far away."

"When will you see them again?" I asked.

"November, maybe," she said, "after we pick the apples. But Manuel says there could be more work after that. Not here, at a different farm."

Luisa not here, at a different farm. I didn't want to think about that. Instead, I asked, "What about school?"

"I will go back, Joe, someday." There was sadness in her voice, but also determination. "My family, when we save enough, we will all come here and be citizens. I will go to school, and so will my sisters. This is my dream."

"That will be good," I said.

"But sometimes I get scared. I think of the bad things that could happen. So I tell myself, *Tú puedes*—You can do it."

"*Tú puedes*," I repeated, liking the sound of it. I wanted it to be true. "*Tú puedes*."

"Thank you, Joe," she said, and I could hear the smile in her voice.

"Hey, I never asked you. Did Manuel like the shorts you gave him?"

"Oh, yes! He doesn't put them on for working, so you do not see him in them. But he wears them all the other times. They are nice, Joe. Very cool!" she said, turning to me and laughing.

I laughed, too, and suddenly our hands were touching and our faces were so close they were almost touching. Her breath was warm and she smelled of something clean and lemony, and before I knew it, my lips were on her lips and we were kissing. I didn't know I was going to do it. I didn't think I knew *how* to do it, but we were kissing. Then, just as suddenly, it was over. We didn't say anything; we just looked at each other. Her eyes were wide and searching in the darkness.

The door of one of the trailers opened, sending a shaft of light across the grass.

"Luisa?"

It was Manuel.

"Luisa!" he called. *"¿Dónde estás?"*

"Estoy aquí," she answered. Then to me she whispered, "I'd better go." She gave my hand a squeeze. *"Hasta mañana.* I'll see you tomorrow."

"Okay," I whispered, squeezing back. *"Hasta mañana."*

"I'm coming, Manuel," she said, rising to her feet. I stood up, too. As she crossed the yard, she said, "I was talking to Joe."

I stepped out of the shadows and called hello. Manuel peered in my direction for a moment, then raised his hand in a wave. I watched as they talked for a minute before going inside.

When I stepped up onto our porch, the phone was ringing. It was my parents.

"Yes," I told them, "everything here is fine."

I could feel a grin that seemed to be permanently plastered on my face. "Everything's going great."

22

It was close to ten o'clock, and I was about to brush my teeth and hit the sack when I heard a horn honking out in the driveway. I went to the window and looked out, but all I could see was the taillights of a car heading up our driveway toward the barns and trailers. I raced down the stairs and out the door, wondering what the heck was going on.

I ran after the car and watched, stunned, as it careened around the circle out in front of the crew's trailers. In a scene that seemed familiar and unreal at the same time, I heard a faint *pop-pop-pop*, followed by laughter and shouted words I couldn't quite make out. The car drove twice around the circle, then headed back down the drive toward me. A light came on in front of Manuel's trailer, and I was able to see the car distinctly. It wasn't one of the two vehicles from the previous late-night joyride. It was a red SUV.

I stood in the middle of the drive as the car headed toward me. At the last minute, I had to jump out of the way as it skidded to a stop near me. Through the passenger side window I saw Randy, grinning with excitement. Beyond him, in the driver's seat, sat Tony.

"Hey, José," said Randy. "*¿Qué pasa?*"

I stared at his smug, smiling face, and I felt so furious

and so—so *flabbergasted* I could barely speak. At last I managed to say, "What are you *doing* here?"

"We were out cruising around," he answered. "So we thought we'd come by and give you and your *amigos* a little thrill."

"What were those explosions?" I asked tightly.

Tony laughed. "*Explosions?* Listen to him." He laughed again.

"Chill out, José," said Randy, laughing along with Tony. "Those were just some little firecrackers left over from the Fourth." He paused, looking at my face. "Come on, man, would you relax? You said your parents were going away, so we were just messing around. It was a *joke.*"

I heard footsteps approaching, crunching on the small stones of the drive. It was Manuel. He stopped a few feet away, looking at us with an expression that seemed both wary and challenging. "These are your friends?" he asked, in a low voice.

I turned from him to Randy and back to Manuel again. His question hung in the air, waiting to be answered. I thought about it. Then I stared right into Randy's face and gave my answer. "No."

Randy looked surprised for a second. Then he smiled scornfully and shook his head. In a pitying voice he said, "You are such a loser."

I kept my eyes on him, and continued speaking to

Manuel. "They were just leaving," I said. "And they won't be back."

Tony laughed, gunned the engine, and pulled away, spewing gravel. Randy turned back and called out the window, "*Hasta la vista*, loser."

They made a right onto the county road, and I watched the car until its taillights disappeared. I turned back to Manuel, and neither of us spoke for a minute. Then I gestured toward the trailers and said, "Is everybody okay?"

He shrugged and nodded.

"No damage?" I asked.

He shook his head and looked away, and I wished I'd asked the question differently. Maybe no property had been broken or smashed, but we both knew there was more than one kind of damage people like Randy and Tony could cause. I wanted to explain to Manuel about Randy, about how for a long time I'd considered him my friend without really thinking about why. But Manuel was already turning to leave.

I stood there until he reached the trailer and the light went out. I remained for a long time, thinking.

Unless Randy pushed it, I wasn't likely to run into him for the rest of the summer. I knew he could make my life difficult when we went back to school, and, knowing Randy, he probably would. But that wasn't what was bothering me.

What had just happened was partly my fault. If I

hadn't had to go bragging about my parents leaving me home alone, Tony and Randy would never have come. All the happiness I'd felt after being with Luisa had drained away. Every time we came closer together, it seemed that something happened to push us apart again. Sometimes I felt as if the gulf between Luisa and me was as wide as the Rio Grande and just as treacherous to cross.

23

I spent a lot of the night tossing and turning and planning what to say to the crew about Randy and Tony. As the "boss," I felt I owed them some kind of explanation or reassurance. It was easy to picture Dad taking charge and saying just the right thing, but I had trouble imagining myself doing the same.

I could feel the crew's eyes on me when I walked out to meet them at the truck the next morning. Some of the guys looked down when I got closer, but Luisa gazed straight at me, waiting.

"Is everybody okay?" I asked first.

There were nods and murmurs of assent.

"Good. About those guys last night," I began. "I know them from school. They're jerks. They thought it would be a big joke to drive through here and give us a scare. I don't think they'll try it again, but if they do, I'll call the police."

At the mention of police, Luisa's eyes widened in alarm. "No, Joe," she said. "No police."

"I meant I'd call them to report Randy and Tony," I explained quickly.

"I know what you meant, Joe," she answered. "But is better not to have the attention of the police now. You see?"

Her eyes implored me to understand, and I did. Luisa, Rafael, and Frank had reason to be leery of the law. It was part of being illegal aliens, this need to remain in the shadows, to be invisible even as they worked in plain sight. Instead of comforting Luisa, I'd made things worse.

"Okay," I said. "No police, then."

Luisa smiled. "Manuel said you told those boys to stay away."

I nodded cautiously.

"So we will hope they do as you say," she said with a little shrug. "And that the others will not come back, either."

Everybody murmured in agreement, and began to climb into the truck.

"Okay, then," I said, grinning with relief. "Let's go to work."

We began weeding the big cabbage field in the far west corner of the farm. It was bordered on one end by the county road that led to the next town over. On both sides were cornfields. One was ours and the other belonged to

Tom Matthews. At the back edge of the cabbage field was a big stand of woods, which was also our property.

That morning we started at the road, and by late afternoon we had almost reached the woods. We were going to finish the field by quitting time. Now that we'd talked about it in the light of day, Randy and Tony's visit seemed more idiotic than frightening. Tomorrow was Sunday, and nobody was planning to work. Everybody was in a good mood. Even Manuel seemed to have lightened up that afternoon. At least he wasn't giving me any dirty looks.

As for me, I had begun to feel pretty terrific again. There was no way to talk privately to Luisa with all the guys around, but I managed to stay close enough to her as we moved down the rows so that I could catch her eye, smile, or pull a funny face to make her laugh.

I was at the end of a row, looking forward to getting a drink of water from the truck. Thinking Luisa might be thirsty, too, I glanced over to the next row where, a minute before, Luisa had been hoeing alongside me. She stood, rigid and unmoving. I was suddenly reminded of the fawn that she had discovered hiding in the hedgerow, its instinct telling it to freeze when danger approached and let its natural camouflage protect it. But Luisa, in her red baseball hat and yellow T-shirt, hardly blended into our surroundings.

The hoe fell from her hand to the ground. Even as I turned in the direction she was looking, I knew what I would see. Parked on the county road were a white car and a white van, both bearing the green insignia of the border patrol. Entering the field and walking quickly toward us were four uniformed men.

For a time that seemed much longer but was surely only a few seconds, the whole world was absolutely still and silent. Then the crew began yelling in Spanish and, before I could quite take in what was happening, Luisa, Rafael, and Frank were off and running into the woods.

I looked back at the officers, who were also running now. They'd only just started into the field, and were still maybe a quarter of a mile away. But they were coming fast, drawing their pistols as they ran.

"No!" I shouted.

When I turned to the woods again to warn Luisa and the others, they were gone.

Out on the road, the white van was pulling away. Some of the officers must have stayed behind and were no doubt heading around the big country block, which was a mile and a half to two miles on each side, hoping to intercept the runaways on the far side of the woods.

Manuel, Gilberto, Carlos, Jorge, David, Antonio, and I stood where we were, helplessly waiting. Soon the men approached, panting and perspiring.

"Where are they going?" one of them called gruffly. It was the same man who had done the talking before. His face was red and very angry looking, and he was speaking to me. One other guy stayed with him, and the other two ran into the woods.

"I don't know," I answered.

"You'd better tell us, if you know," he warned.

"I don't know," I said again, which was the truth. But what if I had known? Why should I tell him? Last time he had told me that none of this was my business.

"It's a mistake for them to run, you know," he said. "We'll find them, and it will go worse for them." He shook his head with frustration. "We gave them a chance. They should have taken it."

"Why don't you just leave them alone?" I burst out. "They're not hurting anybody, they're—" I was shouting now, and my voice was cracking and I was on the verge of tears, but I didn't care. "They're *hoeing cabbage, that's all.*"

There was a silence. Then the man let out a big sigh, looked at the other officer, and shook his head. To me he said, "We don't make the rules, kid. We're just doing our jobs."

Then he turned to Antonio, probably assuming that he was the crew boss because he was the oldest. "Where are they going?"

Antonio shrugged. *"No sé."*

"Yo no sé," said each of the others.

"Nobody knows nothin', is that right?" The officer put his pistol back in the holster and placed his hands on his hips. None of us spoke for a minute or two, as we all watched the two officers who had gone into the woods come back out and head our way.

"Gone," one of them reported in a flat voice.

The guy who seemed to be in charge looked annoyed. "All right," he said disgustedly. "Let's go." He reached into his pocket and handed me a card. "Call that number if they show up, or if you see them or hear anything, understand?"

I nodded without looking at him. Yes, I understood. That didn't mean I'd agreed to do it.

They turned and walked back across the field, and the crew and I stood without speaking until they reached the van and climbed in. The van pulled away, and disappeared.

The whole thing seemed utterly unreal. The sun continued to beat down, making the long rows of cabbage shimmer with light and heat. The smells of the chopped weeds and the freshly turned earth, the sounds of the crows calling and the breeze sighing from the trees were just the same. Yet everything was different. Luisa was gone. Rafael and Frank were gone. There had been ten of us, and now there were seven.

"What should we do?" I said, and my voice sounded high and scared. I tried to make myself calm down. But I had so many questions. "Where did they go? Do you know? *What do we do now?*"

Manuel looked me straight in the face for a long moment. His dark eyes were piercing. I had the feeling he was sizing me up, deciding whether or not he could trust me. Finally he answered. "Right now, we do nothing."

I opened my mouth to protest, but he held up his hand to stop me.

"They will be watching."

I swallowed.

"We act like always. Everything normal, *comprende*?" Manuel's fierce gaze swept us all. "We finish here with the cabbage. We go back like always, we eat. Carlos and Jorge, you shoot the basketball, we watch the television."

I couldn't believe this. *What about Luisa?* I wanted to scream. *Where is she? What is she going to do?*

"We wait," said Manuel.

"Until when?" I couldn't help asking.

"Do you want to help Luisa?" Manuel asked quietly.

"Yes!" I shouted.

"Then do nothing. Until I tell you. Is better this way, *comprende*?"

I felt like yelling, *I don't understand any of this!* Instead, I tried to think. After a moment I said, "But I can't do nothing. I've got to tell Uncle Bud or somebody what's going on. He'll know what to do. He can help."

"No." Manuel's voice was very soft now, very firm. "Your uncle Bud, if he knows something, he must tell the *migra*. Just like you are supposed to do. Is better if you don't know. Is better if you don't tell him or anybody."

But this was too big to keep secret. "I have to call my dad and tell him," I said. "I have to."

"What can he do?" Manuel asked forcefully.

"He—" I paused, then admitted, "I don't know."

"Please, Joe." There was a desperation in Manuel's voice I had never heard before. "Help us. Just wait. I am begging you."

I looked back at Manuel, at the naked pleading in his face. "All right," I heard myself say. "I'll wait."

It was the longest afternoon of my life, far longer than the first days I'd spent hoeing cabbage or picking strawberries. Mental torment, I was discovering, was worse than physical pain. One minute I was filled with fear for Luisa and the others. Where were they? Had they already been captured and taken to jail? Or were they hiding in the woods, or in the high corn, or in an irrigation ditch somewhere? Then I'd be assailed by doubt. Shouldn't I be doing *something*? But what? There was so much I didn't understand.

I told myself that Manuel knew a lot more about what was happening than I did. He was Luisa's cousin, the person who had promised her father he would take care of her. I had to assume he knew what was best for her, and he was asking me to wait, to do nothing, for Luisa's sake. He was crew boss, the person Dad and Mom trusted to watch over the farm. I'd have to trust him, too. More important, I had to trust the little voice inside me that said that, no matter what, helping Luisa was what I had to do.

I know we finished hoeing the field, although I don't really remember doing it. As we drove back to the barn, I worried that one of my uncles would already be there and would see that some of the crew were missing, or that the white van would be waiting in the driveway. But nothing seemed at all out of the ordinary.

When we got out of the truck, there was an awkward moment when we all stood looking at one another, not knowing what to do. Manuel spoke softly to Jorge, Carlos, David, Gilberto, and Antonio. "We go home, eat dinner, act like always."

Then he turned to me. "You, also, Joe. Act normal, like nothing is wrong."

"Okay," I said, "but—"

"Don't come over to the trailer or call. Just wait," he said.

"Until when?"

"Until dark."

24

"Just wait." It sounded so simple. But waiting and not doing anything except trying to act "normal" was one of the hardest things I've ever done.

To my surprise, I fooled everyone. Mom usually had radar for anything unusual that was going on. When she called that evening, I kept expecting her to say, "Joe? What's wrong? You sound funny." But she didn't seem to notice that I was acting odd, if I was. She told me all about what was going on with the relatives, and I said hello to Meg, LuAnn, and Grandma and Grandpa Olmstead. Then Dad got on and asked me how things were going.

I didn't see any point in mentioning the incident with Randy and Tony. It seemed to have taken place a long time ago. What I really wanted to do was blurt out everything that had happened that afternoon and have Dad take over. But I remembered my promise to Manuel. I remembered, too, that this was my chance to prove to Dad— What exactly was I proving? That I could be trusted to do the right thing? Or that I could make a big, fat mess? If only I knew.

"Everything here is okay," I said, trying to sound nonchalant and wondering if Dad was buying it. "The weather's good. We finished the berries. I handed out the checks. Everybody's taking tomorrow off."

And that was it. Dad said they'd try to get in around three or so the following afternoon, and hung up. Later my aunts and uncles checked in, too. It amazed me, really, that I could hide my fear and nervousness from the people who knew me best.

I microwaved a frozen pizza, but I was way too keyed up to eat it.

"Wait until dark," Manuel had told me. The words kept repeating in my brain, making me more and more uneasy. Was there a plan? If so, what could it have to do with me?

"They will be watching," he had said. Just the thought of that gave me the creeps. Was it possible they were watching right then? I tried to look normal and take a bite of pizza. It tasted like dry cardboard and I spit it into a napkin.

Darkness came slowly. I turned on some lights—that was normal, right? I turned on the TV—normal, normal. I stared at it with no idea of what I was seeing.

I waited until long after dark. Every once in a while, I checked the time. Ten o'clock. Ten twenty-five. Eleven-ten. By midnight, I knew exactly what people meant when they said they were about to jump out of their skin.

Where the heck was Manuel? I remembered the long, searching look he'd given me that afternoon, when I'd felt he was deciding whether or not he could trust me. Maybe he had decided he couldn't, that it was too risky to let Little Boss in on the plan.

Was that what was going on? Was he just humoring me, telling me to wait, to sit tight, to do nothing? Don't call, don't come over, don't you want to help Luisa? Yes, I wanted to help Luisa! So what was I doing sitting on my butt in front of the TV while she was out there somewhere hiding or running for her life? Or already in jail?

I'm out of here, I thought.

"They will be watching." Okay. I'd have to make sure there wasn't anything for them to see.

I left the television on and went up to my bedroom,

where I put on black jeans, a long-sleeved dark shirt, and my navy blue New York Yankees hat. Remembering Luisa's brightly colored clothing, I grabbed a couple of dark T-shirts and stuffed them into my backpack, just in case. I took a flashlight from the junk drawer in the kitchen and put that in the pack, too.

My family almost always used the kitchen door rather than the official front door of our old farmhouse. The porch light was on outside the kitchen, but the front of the house was dark. That was where I slipped out. Stepping into the shelter of the big hydrangea bushes in the yard, I stood still to listen and look around.

There was a breeze rustling through the trees, which would help to hide any little noises I made. But it would also mask the sounds of anyone else who was around. I listened again, staring hard into the darkness, but heard and saw nothing suspicious. A car passed on the road, followed a short time later by another, but they seemed to be traveling at normal speeds. There were the night sounds of insects and tree frogs and, every once in a while from the direction of the crew's quarters, the faint noise of the television.

Avoiding the part of the yard that was lit by the porch light, I crept through the shadows of the trees, crossed the driveway in the darkness between the barn and the house, and moved toward the trailers. I was scared and jumpy, and, at the same time, part of me felt ridiculous sneaking around in the dark like some sort of spy on my own farm.

I didn't even know what I was doing: I only knew I had to do something or I was going to go crazy.

I stole up to the trailer where Manuel stayed and peered through the open window, which made me feel even more like a creepy weirdo. But I needed to know what was going on. Inside, the TV was playing, but no one was watching it. Manuel was on the phone, listening, nodding, and occasionally speaking in Spanish, his face very serious. Jorge, Gilberto, David, Carlos, and Antonio were sitting around the room, watching him anxiously.

I realized when I didn't see her that I'd held out a tiny hope that Luisa and the others had come back. But that was impossible. They could never come back, not to this farm.

Manuel hung up the phone and quickly explained to the others what he had learned. From the expressions on their faces, it wasn't good news. In the silence that followed, I tapped very lightly on the window screen.

Everyone inside froze for a second, looking at one another as if to say, "Did you hear that?" I tapped again. Gilberto came to the window and peered out warily.

"It's me," I whispered. "Joe."

He turned to the others and said, "It's Little Boss."

I heard Manuel mutter something in Spanish that sounded as if it might be a swear word.

Too bad, Manuel, I thought angrily. *I'm here and I want to know what's going on.*

He pointed to the back of the trailer, and I went

around to the rear door. He opened it slightly and I stepped inside. We stared at each other for a moment, neither speaking a word.

"I told you—" he began.

But this time I cut him off. "Listen, Manuel, I did what you told me. I didn't tell my dad or my uncles or anybody. I waited, but I'm sick of waiting. I could be in big trouble over this, so you'd better tell me: *What's going on?*"

Manuel ran his hands back through his hair and held them there for a minute, as if he was trying to keep his head from exploding. Finally, he let out a long breath and answered me.

"There is a farm to the north, near Sodus, where Luisa and the others can go and be safe. We know this from Ginny. She helps people when trouble like this comes.

"I know where Luisa and the others are now," he went on, watching me intently as he spoke. "If the patrol didn't find them."

"How do you know?" I asked.

"We decide this before, just in case, after the *migra* come the first time. We picked the place where they will hide until we can come for them."

So there had been a plan all along. "Where?" I asked.

He didn't answer the question, but kept on talking quickly, agitatedly. "But now, is trouble. I keep trying to call Ginny, but she is no answer. If I drive"—he gestured furiously toward the driveway, where his beat-up old car was parked—"I will be noticed. I am stopped sometimes, anyway, when I do nothing wrong."

I nodded. A beat-up old car with Texas license plates and a Mexican at the wheel was way too conspicuous, especially with the border patrol on the alert. I was beginning to understand.

"So you need somebody to pick those guys up where they're hiding, and drive them to this farm you heard about," I said.

Manuel nodded. "Yes, and any minute the *migra* may come here. Or—"

"I'll drive," I said.

"Maybe they find the hiding place already—" He kept on talking, so upset that I guessed he hadn't even heard me.

"I'll drive," I repeated.

He heard me that time. He stared dumbly.

"You'll have to come with me," I went on. "To show me where to go."

Manuel blinked, recovering himself. "But—you can't drive."

"Sure I can," I said. "You've seen me."

"Yes, but, on the road. You do not have the license."

"Manuel, think about it," I said impatiently. "If we get caught, me not having a license is going to be the least of our worries."

There were a few seconds of silence, while he did seem

to think about that. I didn't want him to think too long, though, because *I* didn't want to think about it. If I did, I might chicken out.

"We don't really have a choice, do we?" I said. "It's me, or nobody."

Maybe it was because he was desperate, and because what I'd said was the truth: there really was no other choice. Whatever his reason, I could almost see Manuel make up his mind—to use me, anyway, if not exactly to trust me. Which, right then, was fine with me. What mattered was to get going before it was too late.

If it wasn't too late already. There was no sense in thinking about that, and I pushed the thought away.

"Meet me at Dad's truck," I said, already reaching for the doorknob. "I know where the keys are." Then I thought of something. "But wait. What if they *are* watching the house? You and I might be able to sneak around, but they'll notice the truck leaving, even if we roll down the drive with the lights off."

The frazzled look returned to Manuel's face, as we both tried to think of a solution to this new dilemma.

"I know!" I cried excitedly. "The old green farm truck is out in the lane by the strawberry field—you know, the last one we picked?"

Manuel nodded eagerly.

"The back's full of straw left over from mulching," I said, thinking as I spoke. "But that's good!" I added triumphantly. "For hiding in. Okay, so I'll go get the keys!"

"Wait," said Manuel, grasping my arm. "Listen. This is what we do. I will go through the woods to where Luisa and the others are hiding. We will come near to the road, you know, the county road number 5?"

I nodded.

"We watch for you."

"Where? It's a long road."

"You know the part where no houses are, where the creek goes under the road, only it is dried up—you know the place?"

"Yeah." I was pretty sure I did, anyway.

"We wait there. You drive—like normal—down the road. If there are other cars, or if you see something you don't like, keep going, come back later. If no one is around, you stop. *Comprende?*"

"Yeah." I thought there must be some more questions I should ask, but I couldn't make my brain come up with them.

"Come"—Manuel thought for a minute—"one hour from now."

"Okay," I said. "Here, take this." I handed him my backpack. "There're some dark clothes and a flashlight."

He nodded his thanks and I stepped out onto the strip of grass between the rear of the trailer and the woods. Keeping to the shadows, I worked my way back to the front door of the house and went inside.

First, I checked the time. It was twelve thirty-five. It would take me only ten minutes or so to get out to where the green truck was parked. Another ten minutes to drive to where Manuel said he'd be waiting . . . that meant I had forty minutes. I decided to make a show of going to bed, for anyone who might be watching.

I walked around shutting out lights, turning off the television, and checking the doors and windows. Then I went up the stairs to my room to wait. Making sure it was absolutely dark behind me, I stood at my bedroom window to keep watch for any sign of slow-moving cars or— to tell the truth, I didn't even know what I was looking for.

The minutes crept by so slowly that I went into my parents' bedroom to make sure my clock hadn't stopped. At last it was time to go.

I felt my way down the stairs and into the kitchen, where we kept a board with the keys to all the cars, trucks, tractors, and farm machinery hanging on little hooks. Because there were so many, Mom had put color-coded tags on them to make it easier to find the key you wanted. The key for the blue van had a blue tag, the red truck had a red tag, and so on. Luckily, we had only one green vehicle. I blessed Mom for being so organized.

Once again, I slipped out the door and into the shadows on the edge of the lawn. This time I kept going, past the trailers and through a stand of woods, until I came out on the lane leading to the field where the truck was parked.

On one side of the lane were strawberry plants, on the other, cabbages. A three-quarter moon had come out, and the acres of cabbage heads shimmered silvery-green in its light. It might have seemed magical if I hadn't been so scared. This wasn't the fun-scary feeling of riding the Mind Eraser, either, but the real, heart-pounding, sickening thing.

I saw the outline of the truck and felt a fresh burst of anxiety. I almost wanted to turn back. Then I thought of Luisa hiding out there in the darkness somewhere.

I checked the truck bed. Good. Under an old tarpaulin were the remains of several bales of hay. There was plenty of room for three people, and the tarp and the straw would provide good cover.

I climbed into the cab. My hand was shaking so badly that I had a hard time getting the key in the ignition. When I managed to turn it, nothing happened. I tried again. Nothing.

Come on, I thought. *Start!*

Sluggishly, the motor turned over once and then died. I turned the key again and pumped the gas pedal up and down the way I'd seen Dad do. This time the engine caught and ran for a couple seconds before it died again.

I screamed silently, *Come on, come on, come on!* I was pumping so hard that when the engine caught this time, it roared to life so loudly I was sure it could be heard all the way to town. Leaving the headlights off, I eased the truck into gear and moved slowly down the lane. My palms were slippery with sweat, and I had to grip the wheel tightly to steer in the deep ruts.

When the lane ended, I stopped. *This is it,* I thought. *Once you drive off the farm, there's no turning back.* I looked both ways; there wasn't a sign of another car. Taking a deep breath, I switched on the headlights and pulled out onto the road.

25

I'd never driven this particular truck before. I had to fumble around and feel for the gears, and they were grinding and the truck was bucking so hard I was afraid of stalling. I'd never driven at night before, either. It was disconcerting not being able to see anything beyond the tunnel carved out of the darkness by the headlights.

It was a good thing there was no one else on the road. I had to get my act together, fast. Anybody watching this performance would know I had no idea what I was doing.

I forced myself to settle down and concentrate. When I reached the first corner, I slowed down for the right-hand turn, but not enough. I nearly lost control, barely missing the ditch on the other side of the road.

I drove down another long, deserted two-mile stretch of farmland, getting used to the steering, even putting the truck into third gear to get a feel for speed. Whoa, too fast. Okay, back to second gear.

At the next corner, I stopped, found the turn signal,

then pulled onto the county road where Manuel and the others would be waiting. As I drove along trying to picture where exactly the dried-up creek went under the road, headlights came up behind me, moving fast, filling the rearview mirror and nearly blinding me. As the car passed me on the left, the driver gave a sharp blast of his horn, scaring me half to death.

"Moron," I muttered. Then I noticed the speedometer: I was going only eleven miles an hour. I couldn't believe it. I'd felt as if I was zooming through the darkness, but I was practically creeping down the road. The speed limit was fifty-five, and would be for most of the hourlong trip to Sodus. I had to drive faster.

But first I had to find the place Manuel had described. Praying that no more cars would come, I continued until I reached the long stretch where there were no farm-houses. I was pretty sure the creek bed was coming up and I was about to pull over, when a car came over the rise toward me. I panicked for a second, then speeded up so I wouldn't look suspicious, and kept on going.

I had passed the spot. I wasn't going to risk stopping and turning around in the middle of the road, that was for sure. There was nothing to do but drive all the way around the seven-mile-long block again. Had Manuel seen me go by? If so, he'd understand what happened.

By the time I came around to the meeting place again, I had calmed down and felt a little more in control. I slowed, pulled onto the shoulder, and stopped, scanning the moonlit shapes of bushes and overgrown weeds. *Where were they? Was I too late? Had they been caught? Or was I in the wrong place, after all?*

Then, suddenly, dark shapes emerged from the shadows. I felt the truck shaking, and in the rearview mirror I could see people climbing into the rear bed. There were a few muffled whispers and someone—Manuel, I assumed—arranged the tarp. Then the passenger door opened, and Manuel was in the seat beside me.

"Okay," he said. "Go."

"You found them," I said stupidly, pulling onto the road once again. "Is she—is everybody—all right?"

Another stupid question, I knew. They were alive, they were here in the truck and not in jail, but how could they be all right?

Manuel nodded tersely in answer, but I could tell his mind was already moving ahead. "You know the road we want?" he asked. "Is called route 14."

"Yeah," I said.

"We go north."

"Okay," I said. But my heart had begun to race again. I'd been on route 14 zillions of times, but I had never been the one driving. There were lots of different ways to get there, and most of them led through town. I wanted to avoid the brightly lit streets, the traffic lights and stop signs—and the police station, *for crying out loud*—in town.

"Wait a second. Let me think." I pictured the different

routes in my mind, finally settling on one that would get us there on mostly country roads. They'd be more populated than the one we were on, but at least we'd avoid going through the streets in the center of town.

There was hardly any traffic at that time of the night, which was good, in a way. But being one of the few cars on the road made me feel even more conspicuous. I felt as though a big red arrow hung over us, flashing out the words "Alert! Unlicensed Driver! Illegal Aliens!"

I sensed Manuel fidgeting beside me, and figured he was feeling the same paranoia.

"Can't you drive faster?" he said finally. "You know, like *normal*."

I looked at him and then at the speedometer. Oh, man. He was right. I was doing only twenty-five, and still it felt really fast to me. I was going to have to concentrate every second on driving "like normal."

Except that there was nothing normal about what we were doing.

After an excruciating stretch of time, we reached state route 14 and headed north toward the town of Sodus. Although the road mostly passed through farmland, there were a few small villages along the way, where the speed limit went from fifty-five to thirty. Perfect places for getting busted.

Then we got to the town of Lyons, which I'd forgotten about completely. It was pretty big, and the streets were all lit up. There were people everywhere even though it was around two o'clock in the morning. Why weren't they all home in bed? I wondered crankily. There were cops everywhere, too, which didn't help me to relax one bit.

By the time we got through Lyons I was a wreck, trying to keep my eyes on the road ahead, in the rearview mirror, and on the speedometer. I couldn't seem to get a handle on the speed thing. I felt as if I was going way too fast for the amount of control I had, and still I'd discover I was going too slowly.

The whole time, part of my mind was focused on Luisa—the others, too, but mostly Luisa—in the back of the truck. She had to be uncomfortable and scared and—

Just drive, I told myself.

Adding to my worry were all the deer that came out at night to feed in the fields. From time to time, I'd see their dim shapes or the green glow of their eyes shining in the headlights as they browsed by the road. Once, three of them jumped out of nowhere to race across the road in front of us. I slammed on the brakes and we squealed to a stop and stalled.

I sat for a moment, my heart doing flip-flops. I'd seen what hitting a full-sized deer could do to a truck. The last thing we needed was a crash. I imagined police cars and tow trucks arriving at the scene, and shuddered as I turned the key in the ignition and started up again.

Route 14 went right up to the edge of Lake Ontario. There were lots of big fruit orchards up that way, and I guessed that we were heading for one of them. As we neared the lake, Manuel began peering at road signs.

"Turn here," he said suddenly. "*Derecha*—to the right."

We turned several more times, passing through row after row of fruit trees that grew right up to the side of the road. We came to a sign that said ALDERMAN ORCHARDS— APPLES, PEACHES, CHERRIES—SINCE 1942, passed a big roadside stand, then a house and some barns. About a quarter mile farther, a dirt road led off to the left.

"Here," said Manuel tensely, pointing for me to take the dirt road. "Turn off the lights."

Slowly, we lurched along the rutted lane. I was thankful for the moonlight, which allowed me to see pretty well once my eyes adjusted. Ahead was a clearing with a semicircle of cabins, a few trailers, several cars and trucks, some lawn furniture and a picnic table, and a pole with a plastic gallon jug hanging from a rope.

A light shone from the window of one of the cabins. As we pulled to a stop, the door of the cabin opened, and a man walked toward us, stopping at my window and peering in.

"Manuel?" he said uncertainly.

I pointed to the passenger seat and leaned back so he could see Manuel beside me.

"You are Angelo?" asked Manuel.

"*Sí.*"

"*Bueno.*"

They began talking rapidly in Spanish, and I couldn't follow what they said. Manuel got out of the car, so I did, too. I helped him pull off the tarp that covered the truck bed, and Luisa, Rafael, and Frank sat up, pulling straw from their hair and looking around.

Luisa was wearing some of the dark clothing I had given Manuel. In the moonlight, her eyes looked huge and frightened.

I couldn't help it. I whispered her name. "Luisa!"

"Hi, Joe," she answered, just as quietly. Then she smiled, but I could see the strain on her face.

I nodded hello to Rafael and Frank, and though they smiled, too, they looked anxious and exhausted.

The truth was, I felt like jumping into the truck bed and hugging all three of them, I was just so glad to see them.

There was more rapid Spanish from Angelo, and Luisa and the guys climbed out of the truck. We all stood for a minute, while Angelo explained something to them. I was dying to know what was going on, but I knew enough to keep my mouth shut.

What's going to happen now? As soon as the question crossed my mind, it was answered. Angelo looked at Luisa and pointed to one of the cabins, then he looked at Frank and Rafael and pointed to another.

And that was it. It was time to go. Manuel and the two men hugged each other, shook hands, and hugged again. Then Luisa threw her arms around Manuel. Crying softly, she whispered to him in Spanish. He nodded over and over, as he squeezed her hard. Then he stared into her face for a long moment before letting her go.

It was all happening so fast. I was close to tears myself when Rafael took my hand and shook it.

"*Gracias,*" he said. "*Por todo. Vaya con Dios,* Joe."

"You, too," I answered, realizing at that moment how much I was going to miss Mula.

Then Frank took my hand. "*Muchas gracias,* Joe," he said.

"*De nada,*" I answered, using some of the little Spanish I knew.

"*Eres un verdadero amigo,*" he said, still shaking my hand.

I was suddenly all choked up. I wanted to tell him how much I'd enjoyed working with him, but I couldn't think how to say it. "*Adiós, amigo,*" I said instead.

He gave my shoulder a little punch and with a last grin from under his baseball cap said, "Go, Yankees!"

I laughed and echoed, "Go, Yankees!"

Then I turned to face Luisa. I couldn't help it. As soon as I looked into her face, I took her in my arms. I felt her tears when her cheek touched mine.

"Luisa," I whispered. There was so much I'd have liked to say, but there was no time and I didn't have the words.

"Joe, I will not forget you," she said, "or what you do for us, not ever."

"Shhh," I murmured. "I didn't do anything." There was

something important I needed to say. "Remember what you told me?" I said. "About coming back with your sisters and going back to school someday?"

I could feel her nod.

"*Tú puedes,*" I said softly into her hair. "You can do it. You will do it. I know it."

Angelo spoke sharply then, and I knew he was impatient for Luisa and the others to be safely inside and for Manuel and me to leave.

"Goodbye, Luisa."

She pulled away from me and put a finger to my lips. "No. Not goodbye, Joe. *Hasta luego.* But not goodbye."

Until later. I knew what the words meant, and I wanted to believe that I would see her again.

She turned to go.

"Wait!" I cried. I ran back to the passenger side of the truck and pawed through the glove compartment. *Please,* I prayed silently, *let it be there.* My fingers closed around a long narrow shape—yes, a syringe! I went back and pressed it into Luisa's hand. "You watch for hornets," I said, holding her face in my hands. "Keep this with you. All the time, okay?"

She nodded. I kissed her gently.

"Luisa!" Manuel whispered loudly. "You must go!"

"Thank you, Joe," she said, and she was smiling and crying at the same time. "I had to leave Señor Oso behind. You give him to Meg, all right? Until I come back."

Señor Oso? For a second I hesitated, feeling confused.

Then I remembered. "The panda bear! Sure, I'll give him to Meg."

Luisa began to walk away, then turned to say, "My dress! The one my mother sewed." She faltered, and my chest ached for her.

"I'll keep it for you," I promised. "Until you come back."

"Luisa!" Manuel was pushing her now toward where the others had headed.

And then she was gone. They all were gone. Manuel and I got into the truck and drove out the way we had come.

We didn't talk for a long time after that. It wasn't because of the difference in our languages. I was learning that there are times when it's impossible to find the words for what is in your heart, no matter what language you speak.

We were maybe halfway home—it was hard to tell, because it was dark and I didn't know the road very well, and because my mind was so disoriented from everything that had happened—when I noticed headlights in my rearview mirror. I looked down at the speedometer and saw I was going thirty-five. *You've got to pay attention!* I scolded myself silently. *Why didn't you think to let Manuel drive? Stupid.*

Rather than pulling over right then and switching drivers, I figured I'd wait until whoever it was passed me, as the few other cars that had come from behind earlier had done. But this car hung back, remaining at the same distance from the truck, for what felt like a mile. It was making me nervous.

"Manuel," I said in a low voice, breaking the silence. "There's a car just sitting on my tail back there. What should I do?"

Manuel looked back over his shoulder. Then he looked at the speedometer. "Better to speed up, maybe," he said.

"Okay." I pressed my foot on the accelerator. Then I glanced into the rearview mirror just in time to see a bar of flashing red lights appear across the top of the car and to hear the *whoop-whoop-whoop* of a police car's siren.

26

"Oh, man," I moaned. "Oh, man. I can't believe this. I can't believe this is happening. It's a cop. What do I do? What do I *do*?"

"You have to stop, Joe," Manuel said urgently. "Pull to the side."

"Oh, man," I repeated as I steered the truck to the shoulder and stopped. "We're dead. I'm dead. Oh, man."

The siren went off, but the red lights continued flashing. In the side mirror, I could see the policeman get out of his car. He shone a flashlight around in the back of the truck, even picking up the tarp and looking underneath.

I had a momentary rush of panic, thinking how much worse this would have been had it happened on the way to Sodus instead of now.

It was plenty bad enough now.

The flashlight beam shone through the window on the back of the cab, lighting up Manuel's head and then mine. Then the cop's face appeared at my open window, and the light flashed directly in my face for a second, then went off.

"License and registration, please."

License—forget it. I remembered once when Mom had gotten pulled over for a missing taillight or something. She'd gotten papers out of the glove compartment and handed them to the officer. The door on the dash was still ajar from when I'd gotten the syringe for Luisa. I fumbled around until I felt a little plastic sleeve with some papers inside. I handed them over, and the officer examined them.

"This truck's owned by a James L. Pedersen. Is that you?"

"No, sir," I said. "That's my father."

"And you would be . . . ?"

"Joe. Joe Pedersen, sir."

"This vehicle is registered for farm use only, not for the highway. Did you know that?"

I shrugged.

"May I see your license, Joe?"

There was a pause, while I tried to think of something

I could say that would get me out of this. "I don't have one," I answered at last.

"Do you know why I pulled you over, Joe?" the officer asked.

I shook my head.

"You were going about thirty-five in a fifty-five zone. Now, in my experience that means a driver who is either drunk or very old . . . or else a driver who's young and inexperienced. How old are you, Joe?"

"Fourteen," I mumbled.

"Would you mind getting out of the car for a minute, Joe?"

I opened the door and stood in the glare of the flashing red lights.

"Would you mind taking a little walk down the yellow line by the shoulder of the road there, Joe?"

I knew that he was watching to see if I could walk straight, and that made me even more nervous than I already was. I stumbled once, and was terrified he'd think I was drunk as well as underage and unlicensed. But he seemed satisfied.

"Okay, Joe, you can come on back here."

When I was standing before him once again, he said quietly, "So, Joe. What are you doing out at"—he checked his watch—"close to three in the morning, driving without a license?"

I shrugged. "I don't know, sir."

"Do your parents know where you are?"

"They're out of town."

"And they let you stay home alone?"

"Yeah," I said. I didn't see any point in trying to explain.

"And so you decided to go for a little joyride with your friend here?" He pointed into the cab at Manuel, who hadn't moved or said a word since we'd been stopped.

Joyride? I thought. *If you only knew.*

I shrugged again.

"Did you boys get into any trouble tonight?"

"No, sir."

"Just out riding around, is that it?"

"Yes, sir."

He looked right at me for a minute, and I was surprised to see something like kindness or understanding in his eyes. I noticed the name tag on the pocket of his uniform. Sergeant H. V. Wellman.

"Well, Joe, we can't allow fourteen-year-old boys to be out driving around. It's against the law, I'm sure you're aware of that."

"Yeah," I answered, in a voice so low he might not even have heard me.

"I could take you down to the station now, book you, and keep you until your parents come back."

He paused, maybe to give me time to think about that. I pictured myself sitting in a jail cell, and imagined the look that would be on Dad's face when he came to get me. I was dead.

"That could keep you from getting your night license, even when you are sixteen," Sergeant Wellman went on.

Oh well, I thought, *I'm not going to live to be sixteen, anyway.*

"But I've got a feeling about you, Joe. I'm betting this is your first offense, is that right?"

I nodded.

"Okay. I'm going to make this easier on you than I could, you understand?"

I nodded again, even though I didn't really understand, except that it sounded as if he was going to give me a break.

"What I need you to do, Joe, is promise me you'll never pull another boneheaded stunt like this. What do you say?"

"Yes. I mean, I do. I promise. I won't."

Sergeant Wellman gave me a long, searching look. "Okay," he said. Then he peered into the cab at Manuel. "You, son," he said, "how old are you?"

Manuel looked startled at being addressed. "Sixteen," he answered.

"You got a license?"

Manuel nodded, reached into his back pocket, and handed over his license.

"Manuel Velarde," the sergeant read aloud, and I realized it was the first time I'd ever heard Manuel's last name.

"I gotta ask," the sergeant said, looking at us curiously. "Why was Joe here driving, when you've got a license?"

It was a logical question, but there was no way we could answer it with the truth: on the trip up we were afraid of getting caught for transporting illegal aliens, and on the way back we were too freaked out to think of trading places.

"My dad's truck," I said with a shrug.

"I see," said Sergeant Wellman. If he suspected there was more to the story than that, he decided to let it go. "All right, Manuel, I'd like you to switch places with Joe and drive this truck home. Where do you live?" he asked, turning to me.

I explained where the farm was.

"You live at the farm, too?" the officer asked Manuel.

"Yes."

The sergeant nodded. "Okay, then. I'm going to follow you boys home in the cruiser. First, I'm going to have to write you a ticket, Joe, for being underage and driving without a license in an unregistered vehicle. I won't make you go to the station now, but you are going to have to appear in family court with your parents, and there's a chance you'll get a pretty hefty fine."

He went back and sat in the police car, writing out the ticket, I guessed. Manuel and I switched places and waited, too dazed and tired to talk.

Sergeant Wellman handed the ticket through the window, and I placed it on the seat without looking at it.

The sergeant told Manuel to drive home carefully. He followed us, with the flashing red lights mercifully turned off, all the way into the driveway at the farm. The windows in the crew's quarters glowed with light, and I pictured the rest of the guys inside, anxiously waiting for Manuel to get back.

The sergeant told me there were instructions on the ticket for what my parents and I had to do. Before he left, he said, "Now, don't make me sorry I gave you a break, Joe."

"No, sir."

Manuel and I stood in the driveway for a moment, watching the police car until it disappeared. "Well," I began, "I—"

But Manuel interrupted. His face in the dim light looked very serious. "I don't know—how to say—except, thank you. I will tell your father when he comes back, it was not your fault. I—"

"No," I broke in. "You don't have to say anything. I wanted to go. I knew what I was doing."

Manuel looked right at me, and I almost had the feeling he was really seeing me for the first time. "We are—all of us—very grateful," he said rather formally. Then he reached out to shake my hand. "Thank you, Boss."

I went inside and climbed the stairs to my room. I put

the ticket on the bureau and fell onto the bed, more tired than I'd ever been. It wasn't until the moment right before I slipped from consciousness that I realized Manuel had called me Boss.

27

I woke up hot and sweaty, and my room was filled with blazing sunshine. I closed my eyes quickly to block out the glare, along with the vague sensation that something terrible had happened that I didn't want to face. Dim memories passed through my mind, filled with darkness and furtive movement and flashing red lights.

Red lights. A police car. Luisa's face, her eyes huge and dark with fear. A nightmare?

I opened one eye and saw the ticket sitting on my bureau. No, not a nightmare. I opened the other eye, letting the pain of the blinding sun jolt me to full awareness. The events of the previous night washed over me all at once, and I sat straight up in bed. I glanced at the clock: It was after one in the afternoon. No wonder the sun was beating in so ferociously.

I let my mind linger on everything that had happened the night before. And the strange thing was, once I really thought about it all, I felt great.

When Dad got home and saw the ticket and found out what I'd done, I'd be in deep, deep trouble. I'd have to endure the look of disappointment on his face, watch him set his jaw to control his anger, listen to him say that he knew he should never have trusted me. We'd go to family court, where my father would have to promise to be responsible for me, since it was obvious I couldn't be counted on to take care of myself.

Mom would be all upset, and probably blame herself for leaving in the first place. LuAnn . . . I didn't even want to think about the grief she'd give me, or the smirk on her face when she said, "Joe, I thought I told you not to do anything stupid."

It was going to be a big, fat mess, that was for sure, and I dreaded going through it. But, at the same time, I felt incredibly calm. I knew that what I had done was against the law, and that meant it was wrong. So why did it feel so right? That's what it really came down to. It felt right to have helped Luisa and Rafael and Frank. If I had to pay the consequences, okay. It was worth it.

That feeling of calm stayed with me for the next two hours, until the moment when Mom's van pulled into the driveway.

I heard all about the reunion while I helped my family unload their stuff. When we had everything unpacked, Mom announced that she didn't feel like cooking and suggested we all go out for pizza. Ordinarily, I'd have been the first one in the car. But I didn't want to go out and sit through what was supposed to be a happy, carefree family meal with all that was on my mind.

"Mom? Dad? Before we go out, could we talk for a second?" When LuAnn turned to me, her ears perked with interest, I scowled at her and added, *"Alone."*

"Of course, Joe," said Mom, and a flicker of worry crossed her face. She gave LuAnn a look.

LuAnn sniffed and said, "Come on, Meg. Let's go see if Luisa's around."

I didn't even try to stop them. They'd find out soon enough.

As soon as the kitchen door had closed behind them, I said, "You guys probably ought to sit down."

They did, both of them looking really serious now. "What is it?" asked Dad.

First I told them about Randy and Tony driving through the farm on Friday night.

"What were they thinking?" Mom said, her eyes flashing angrily.

"It was their idea of a *joke*," I said, making a face. "I told them off. I don't think they'll do it again. And I won't be hanging around with Randy anymore."

Mom looked at me thoughtfully for a moment. "Well, good for you, Joe," she said. "That sounds like a very sensible decision." She gave me a little hug.

"But that isn't really what I wanted to tell you," I said.

She looked surprised, and so did Dad. "It isn't?" she asked.

I shook my head and took a deep breath. Beginning with the appearance of the I.N.S. in the cabbage field, I told them the whole story, right through to the end. Well, *most* of the story, anyway. I left out the owner's name and the exact location of the farm where we'd gone.

They stopped me from time to time to ask a question, but mostly they listened. When I had finished, I placed the ticket on the table in front of them and waited. It was hard to tell from the expressions on their faces what they were thinking.

They looked at each other, probably deciding who was going to talk first. Finally, Mom said, "Well. You've had quite a time, haven't you, Joe?" She sounded kind of dazed.

There was no good answer for that, so I didn't say anything.

She went on. "I guess the thing I'm having a hard time with is that you didn't call to tell us—that you didn't tell *anyone*. Why not, Joe? We could have helped you."

"How?" I asked. "You were so far away and it all happened so fast. And Manuel—" I was about to say that Manuel had asked me not to say anything. But I didn't want to make it sound as if I was blaming him. "I mean, I figured that the fewer people who were involved, the better. See, the I.N.S. guy made it sound like if I knew where Luisa and Rafael and Frank were, I had to tell. I thought if you didn't even know they were missing, let alone where they'd gone, there was no way you could get in trouble." I spread my hands as if to display the logic of my thinking, so they could see it and understand.

"I know it was bad to take the truck and drive at night and all that," I went on. "I'm sorry about the ticket and having to go to court, too. I'll pay the fine out of my wages." I paused, then added quietly, "But I'm really *not* sorry about what I did."

There was a long silence, and my heart sank. They didn't understand. I guess I shouldn't have hoped that they would. I turned around, thinking I'd go to my room before I was told to, leaving them to talk over how they wanted to handle my punishment.

"Joe, wait." It was Dad. "Sit down."

I did.

"Give us a minute here," he said. "This is a lot for your mother and me to take in all at once. You've had more time to think about this than we have."

Well, that was the truth.

After what seemed a long pause, he said, "There's no getting around the fact that you broke the law, Joe."

Here comes the lecture, I thought.

"And as the sergeant said, we can't condone that."

"I know," I said glumly.

"And that puts your mother and me in a hard place."

"I know," I said again.

"Because the thing is, laws made by humans aren't always perfect. Sometimes there's another law, a higher law, that we feel we have to answer to."

I nodded, feeling a tiny prickle of hope. What Dad was saying was exactly what I'd been trying to get clear in my own mind.

"The immigration laws are a mess—harmful and misguided in some instances, and just plain silly and contradictory in others. That's my opinion. However, they're still the laws of the land and, as a citizen, I'm bound to obey them. Just as," he added, surprising me with a little smile, "we're bound to obey the rules of the road, even if we don't agree with them. Although in that case, I'm with the powers that be: fourteen-year-olds have no business on the highways."

I had to smile back at that. If he'd seen me the night before, he'd know he was right.

Dad sighed. "Anyway, Joe, the point I'm trying to make is that this is a very complicated thing. As we get older, we realize that there aren't always easy answers when it comes to right and wrong. I can't look my son in the face and say it's all right to break the law. On the other hand, I can't tell you what you did was wrong, either. The fact is, I don't think Luisa and Frank and Rafael belong in jail. I'm glad they're safe."

"I am, too," Mom added softly.

I opened my mouth to breathe a deep sigh of relief. I'd been prepared for their anger and their disappointment, but I hadn't been prepared for this.

"If you had asked my permission ahead of time," Dad went on, "I'd have told you, absolutely, positively *no*. But you didn't ask. Part of me wants to get upset about that, but I can't quite seem to." He stopped and shook his head. "You made your own decision, and I don't imagine it was easy." Then he reached across the table to grasp my shoulder. "Now that it's all said and done, and you and everybody else are safe, I'm going to say this, Joe. I'm proud of you."

28

We were shorthanded the next week, and the crew— what was left of it—and I busted our tails. As I worked, I wondered if the I.N.S. would come back, and one day one of them did. He came to the house, not out to the fields, and talked to Mom and Dad.

The guy told them he didn't make a practice of coming onto people's land and looking for trouble. But in this case, a couple of Mexicans he described as "bad apples" had been involved in a fight at a bar. Somebody had tried to break it up and had gotten badly hurt. The Mexicans had fled, and the I.N.S. was looking for them. It was suspected they'd found work on a local farm in order to stay out of sight for a while. That was why the I.N.S. had first stopped at our place and others, too, hoping to catch them unaware.

Then, when the "bad apples" weren't found, the I.N.S. was under pressure to follow up on every possibility, which was why they came back.

Mom told the officer she was sure Luisa, Rafael, and Frank weren't the ones involved, but that they'd been so scared they'd run away, too. Mom and Dad both were able to look the guy in the eye and say they didn't know where Luisa, Frank, and Rafael were now, because I had never told them.

We hoped we'd seen the last of the I.N.S. for a while.

On the following Sunday, some new workers arrived. Manuel arranged it, don't ask me how. A guy named Silvino came with his wife, Carmen, and her sister, Teresa. A couple weeks later, Hector, Victor, and a guy whose name really was José showed up for the apple harvest.

All of them had papers to show to Mom and Dad. Maybe they were legal papers, maybe not. Maybe they had left another farm the same way Luisa and Frank and Rafael had left ours. Who knew? In the meantime, the fruit and the vegetables ripened and had to be picked.

Mom and Dad and I went to family court, where I promised to be good and they promised to keep an eye on me. I paid the hundred-dollar fine out of my wages.

Not too long ago, forking over that much money would have really bummed me out. I'd have sat down and figured out how many more days I was going to have to work before I could order the Streaker, and how many days that would leave me to ride it.

But the funny thing was, I didn't think about the Streaker anymore. I didn't even want it. The *X-treme Sportz* catalog sat on my bureau for a while, but finally I threw it out. I knew I wouldn't be riding with Randy and Jason and, anyway, I had other stuff on my mind.

I got a raise to $5.50 an hour, which was pretty cool. Dad said Manuel told him that my work had improved and I deserved it. Knowing that was almost as good as having the extra money. I didn't know what I was going to do with it all, but I liked knowing it was in the bank and that I'd earned it.

I thought about Luisa all the time. I spent the long working hours trying to picture her in her new life. I imagined her up on a ladder picking apples, or playing tetherball with the milk jug that hung from the pole in the yard of her new home, wisps of hair falling in her eyes and her long braid flying.

Once, I looked up Alderman Farms in the phone book and dialed the number. When a lady answered, I hung up, feeling foolish.

One evening near the end of July, I was cutting the grass when I saw Manuel walking across the yard toward me. I shut off the mower.

"I thought you like to know," he said, "I have heard from Luisa."

"Really?" I said eagerly. "She called?"

He shook his head. "No, I hear from Ginny. She saw them—Luisa, and Frank, and Rafael."

"So how are they? Are they okay?"

"Yes, Ginny says so. She says their new bosses are nice. Luisa and Frank and Rafael will stay for apples, until the middle of November. They send their greetings to everyone here."

I waited. "That's it?" I asked, wanting to hear more, wanting to hear *anything* about Luisa.

"That's it," Manuel said, and started to go. Then he turned back. "Oh, yes, I almost forgot. There is a message from Luisa for you, also."

"*What?*" I said.

Manuel started to laugh, and I saw that he had been teasing me by holding the news from Luisa until last. "But it doesn't make sense," he said apologetically. "Maybe you no want to hear."

"Just tell me!"

"You sure you want to hear?"

"*Tell me!*"

"Okay. She said"—he drew his words out slowly, tantalizingly—"to say to you that she is looking at the same sky." He gave me a puzzled frown and shrugged. "But you see? I told you. It makes no sense."

I didn't tell Manuel that to me it made perfect, beautiful, wonderful sense. I couldn't have spoken right then, even if I'd wanted to, because my heart felt as if it had risen right up to fill my throat. Instead, I looked at the sky, at the sun that was also shining on Luisa in Sodus. I closed my eyes and let it warm my face.

Later that night, I sat under the maple tree and watched the stars come out, and then the moon, and felt Luisa watching them, too.